MW01133276

Remembering
What I Forgot

K. Allen

Memory Care Charge Nurse

© 2017 Gwenlee Publishing

ALL RIGHTS RESERVED. This book contains material protected under International and Federal Copyright Laws and Treaties. Any unauthorized reprint or use of this material is prohibited by law except for brief passages which quote previous printed/published material. Otherwise, no other part of this book may be reproduced or transmitted in any form or by any means, electronic or mechanical, including photocopying, recording, or by any information storage and retrieval system without express written permission from Ken Boring.

© Cover Image: image copyright Kesipun, used under license from Shutterstock.com.

Table of Contents

About the Author

Introduction

As nurse supervisor of a dementia unit, I have learned to comfort those who feel scared, reassure those who are lost, and love those who can no longer control their emotions. On any weekday in late afternoon, I labor with residents who have lost their ability to reason or rationalize and who struggle to remember anything past several seconds.

Caring for them is a formidable challenge, but functioning as a supervisor is only the surface of what I do. My true calling is learning to connect with the person behind the illness. Getting to *know* them isn't always easy but the rewards are priceless; A hug, a laugh, a wink, a dance, a peck on the cheek or simply a grin from ear to ear—all go both ways.

Beyond the disease is a person who still exists. Sometimes I can find them, sometimes it's too late. Patience, compassion and understanding are all prerequisites here but are merely the membrane of my responsibilities as a memory care clinician.

Here we learn many lessons which can greatly benefit us all, so long as we are willing to invest the necessary time and resources. This is one story of many lessons.

*Sometimes you will never know the value
of a moment until it becomes a memory.*

—Dr. Seuss

Tell me and I'll forget,

Show me and I may remember,

Love me and I'll understand.

Chinese Proverb

Jump Start

"He's not breathing!" she cries out.

Bolting into the dining area, I see Calvin laid out next to his table.

"Florence call 911 and you—grab the AED!"

"We called, Shannon went to the Van Gogh for the defibulator!"

"Good, and you're sure he's full code?"

"Yes!"

"Okay, what happened?"

"Shannon said he had been acting funny and then he slid out of his chair."

Florence remained motionless, not sure of what to do and appearing almost scared. Unable to detect Calvin's pulse or respirations, I establish an airway before beginning resuscitation. I instruct her to grab a blood pressure cuff and stethoscope from the wagon when suddenly Shannon rushes in with the defibulator.

We quickly set down the device. Reaching to push the ACTIVATE button, I'm unable to control a tremor of my hand. Following the auditory directive of the

AED, I remove his shirt before attaching the sticky elec-tro- leads to his chest while Florence velcros the cuff around his arm.

"What's for dessert?" I hear from behind me. "Yes-terday they offered an apple cobbler, but honestly, it tasted like cardboard!" I recognize the voices as Molly and Thelma.

"Get these people outta here!" I bark at the staff.

Within seconds the device indicates a shock is needed.

"CLEAR!" I shout placing my trembling finger on a red triangle button labeled SHOCK. Despite having practiced this in dozens of CPR training sessions, I'm a wreck and now my heart pounds. Calvin reacts with a jolt and the computer calls for another surge. Again, I nervously reach for the button.

Molly and Thelma continue. "I wish they had soft ice cream more often . . . that would be nice."

I do my best to tune them out.

"CLEAR!" once more, I give him the juice and he re-sponds with an agonizing jolt and groans. Is he going to make it? The first EMS enters onto the unit and I feel relief. Several residents linger including the Troll, who's staring down one of the paramedics. His tall build and "Tom Brady" looks have her curious, and I can sense she's trying to muster up the courage to pester him. Bursting forth with her walker, she waddles toward him with all the determination of a penguin running for its life.

"What time you gonna give me my pills?" She shouts.

"I don't have your pills ma'am."

"Get her outta here!" I command the aides. "She's in the way!"

"Why do I have to go?" She argues. "I'm just talking to him!"

Bickering, she refuses to depart the area and proceeds to bump Betty, causing her to trip over Calvin and drop to the floor. Several residents head for the exit while the EMS delivers the final shock before preparing Calvin for transport.

Florence and I help Betty to her feet, but she cannot stand. We help her to sit at a nearby table before escorting out the remaining onlookers.

Finally, Calvin has a weak pulse and is breathing on his own. Thank God...I think as I see the butterfly IV needle taped to his hand. I think of the day he arrived. I love him like my dad. I help to secure an O_2 mask onto his face and thank the crew for arriving so quickly.

"No problem." They replied. "We were at the nursing home next door. It was a transport to the hospital, but the old geezer was gone when we got there…coroners on the way."

Helping to empty out the remaining bystanders, I notice Betty looking dazed and confused. Something isn't quite right but I can't put my finger on it. Next I see the Troll following the EMS crew off the unit while insisting on her pills. Shannon quickly intervenes and redirects her to the executive lounge along with Molly and Thelma. Others remained oblivious to the commotion and continued eating.

Suddenly Betty collapses to the floor. Her pulse is rapid and thready. She's perspiring and her breathing has stopped. It dawns on me she must have received a shock when she tripped over Calvin and is now in cardiac arrest! I radio for help and administer rescue breathing. The only set of sticky electro leads left with Calvin, rendering the device useless.

I instruct Florence to redial 911 and Shannon to grab the other AED from the Clinic. Within minutes the room floods again with staff members including "Tom Brady" followed by Shannon who's located the AED. Together we're able to jump start Betty before stabilizing her for transport. Finally, I head for my office where

I document the madness in addition to notifying family members of those transported out.

Today I am the only nurse supervisor on a locked unit, The Rembrandt, and an assisted living complex, the Van Gogh. Together they house over 100 residents. My job entails continual prioritizing of duties such as; medication administration, supervising staff, performing assessments and documenting the resident's conditions. On most days, I operate in survival mode due to staffing shortages. Rarely am I afforded a meal break.

My first exposure to this type of setting was at the Brook Lawn Nursing Home in Glen Bernie, Maryland. The year was 1970. One weekend a month my two older brothers and I would pile into our parents' station wagon to brave the hour-long drive to visit our great Aunt Lizzy, on our mom's side.

Approaching 100, Lizzy basically couldn't see or hear and mumbled throughout our visits. My brothers and I would elicit stares from residents who appeared anxious and at times zombielike. We'd snicker about the appearance of some and pretend not to notice others— while walking faster. Most I remember residents in their beds with looks of despair while others propelled around in wheelchairs.

Dad would be seen checking his watch—with precise timing—before getting *the look* from mom. We all knew *the look*. A senior captain for Eastern Airlines and Lieutenant Colonel in the Army Special Forces, dad was a walking model of self-sufficiently. The self-effacement Brook Lawn forced on him however, dealt a serious blow to his pride. He was never at ease in what he referred to as the *Old Soldier's Home*. The drive home allowed each of us time to process our thoughts. Little was said.

The following spring would be our final visit. Lizzy died in her sleep not long after we'd left her on that blustery Easter Sunday. She was the first person I remember viewing in a coffin and while curious, I was careful not to get *too* close. I remember staring at her face, wondering about death and thinking how she only appeared to be sleeping. What about all of those back at Brook lawn? Weren't they just waiting *their* turn to be in the casket? At least Lizzy was at peace, the others were not.

Entering my cubical-sized office, I'm greeted by our unit mascot, Mr. Robinson, a morbidly obese, emerald eyed tuxedo cat whose neck patch of white fur makes for a near perfect bow tie. Twitching his tail, he rises and gives a faint "meow" as if to say "you're back". He's not only shaped like a bomb; he *is* the bomb around here.

To my knowledge, he's never missed a meal and will gladly massage whatever ankles are necessary for attention but especially for table scraps.

His personality is perfect for our population. Like many animal companions, he's able to communicate his affection with memory-impaired residents who never talk or display any willingness to interact. He's been known to enter closed cabinets, remove unopened boxes of cat food and consume the entire contents before retiring to his favorite rocker. His food has since been locked up and lately there's even been talk of him attending an animal weight watchers class offered on weekends. He may not always make it from the floor to the rocker on his first leap, but he's still one cool cat. A gentle stroke of his back starts his engine, and suddenly I realize how much I've missed him these last few days.

Numerous resident charts litter my desk, most of which will require various tasks such as transcribing new orders, thinning, breaking down, or continued charting. One is stamped ADMISSION and will take hours to complete. The nurse I am due to relieve is attending a Collaborative Care meeting so my status report will come from a twenty-four-hour written communication log.

"Geeze Louise." I whine. "This is gonna take hours."

Clearing an area on my desk, I notice a stack of faxes that need processing and the message light on my phone is flashing. Additionally, I see a memo informing all nurse supervisors that corporate headquarters has eliminated another nurse's aide position and the water is due to be turned off at 8:00 p.m. tonight for repairs.

Opposite my desk is a cork board crammed with notes, memos and phone numbers. A closer look reveals an employee's name ~~Bonnie,~~ along with a handwritten note…QUIT! Lastly, I notice a memo announcing that a fire drill to be held sometime following today's associate stand-up meeting, scheduled for 5 p.m. A term which probably originated somewhere around the turn of the previous century, standup refers to the limited number of chairs available for staff during report.

I've done my best to make it standup comedy but others aren't so easily amused. First come, first serve remains the only way to guarantee yourself a seat. Little has changed with me as well, I always stand.

"What time you going to give me my pills?"

Mr. Robinson and I look up. "Seven o' clock" I answer.

"What was that?"

"Seven o'clock!"

I take a deep breath. Standing before me in her pink,

floral, flannel pajamas is four foot, eleven-inch Sally, affectionately nicknamed "The Troll"; A garden gnome really; a permanent fixture of sorts around here. She sports a jet-black bowl cut with Buddy Holly glasses and razor stubble and will inquire about her pills no less than a dozen times per shift.

"Alright, well don't forget...I'll be in bed," she says with a stern stare.

Sally often uses selective listening and is easily able to do much more for herself than she leads others to believe. She's become somewhat of an expert at knowing how to coerce fellow residents into doing that which she's simply too lazy to do herself. The staff doesn't buy it and fellow residents are intimidated by her "Joe Pesci" demeanor. She's mastered the fine art of attention seeking and beyond. At times, it's comical to watch how convincing she can be while attempting to manipulate others into feeling sorry for her.

She'll have them fetching water from the cooler or instructing others on how to correctly put on her socks and even give up their wheelchair for her. Sally takes manipulation to a whole new level and has even convinced others that she's *sometimes* paralyzed. Most of this behavior, we believe, results out of sheer boredom, in addition to her being a control freak. Although she may suffer from memory impairment, she's much more aware of her true abilities than she's willing to admit and possesses little if no impulse control.

Sally will usually refuse to participate in activities or socialize with others unless *she's* allowed to be the one in charge. She earned the nickname, "The Troll", mostly due to her physical stature but also due to her constant bossiness. Her tenacity remains unmatched by all standards and given time she will find a way of getting under your skin—and she knows it! Like the others here, she didn't come by way of choice and deserves to be provided for and loved like family.

Currently, she is the least of my worries as my admission could be here at any moment and I have nearly a dozen residents who need their medication before the dinner hour. After clearing several phone messages, I finish reviewing the report log, emails and scan my desk for any STAT orders. Stat in medical parlance is short for statim, the Latin word for immediately. Seeing nothing requires instant attention, I head for my medication cart, often referred to as "the wagon." …

Welcome to the wagon, my pharmacy on wheels.
You'll find me in these hallways
either before or after meals.
We have Ativan, diazepam, Lorazepam and more.
Careful what you take as you may end up on the floor.
If it's Colace, Mira lax or Geritol you need
We have all those including Marinol,
today's medical form of weed.

Mother's Little Helper

At the Wagon

Medication administration is a very exacting and tedious task for a nurse, and when attempting to administer to residents with dementia, it can be quite challenging. Some resist nearly any form of care or treatment and to have them swallow a pill is, at times, impossible. Often, I am having to reattempt later which is frustrating as the allotted time-period to dispense is limited.

One option is to alter the way in which to administer, such as crushing the medication and then mixing it in with apple sauce or pudding. This is very monotonous and time consuming and may prove to be ineffective as residents often are suspicious and refuse to accept it. It's imperative that certain residents receive their medication on time to avoid potential behavioral problems. Certain ones can quickly escalate and once they begin to act out, it becomes even more challenging to engage them in any meaningful way.

Unlocking my cart, I notice Emma walking toward me wearing her full-length silver fox which is common for her even though the temperature on our unit is rarely less than 80 degrees. Many seniors here will often *feel* colder than their younger contemporaries simply due to having less subcutaneous fatty tissue. This gradual loss of tissue, which occurs subtly over many years, contributes to both heat loss and dehydration.

"Where have you been handsome...I haven't seen you for months?" Her warm smile is contagious.

"I've been right here waiting for you." I answer with a wink.

We both laugh and have a hug. This occurs almost daily now with Emma as her ability to recall when she last saw me has significantly declined. It's deja vu as she continues to stare at me with her lovable, happy grin. Her diminishing state is a trademark of those afflicted with AD, and is commonly referred to as staging. Lately, her cognitive decline has noticeably worsened and today I know she wanted to call me by name—but just couldn't. Lately her favorite default name for me is "handsome." I love that she chooses to engage me. Knowing I'm her friend is endearing to me. She and the others here give me what I need most—the feeling of knowing I'm wanted.

Emma possesses such a gentle and warm demeanor that I am sometimes overcome with emotion when I see her. Her tall slender build, fake eyelashes and full head of beautiful red hair suggest she no doubt once sported the curves of a pin-up doll. From a distance, she's "Dear Abby." After taking time to compliment her on how nice she looks, I hand her a drink of cold water along with a tiny soufflé cup containing her meds.

"Oh, I've already taken those today." she says with a dubious look.

"Yes, I know...but the doctor wants you to have these in the evening also."

"Well okay, if you say so."

Successful administration is often determined by her mood and whether she decides to trust me; this being true with a few other residents who also reside here. Despite my having known Emma for nearly five years now, she is not always able to remember me as someone she can trust. Quality time spent socializing with her and others is one thing I relish but am rarely afforded. Consistent interaction is vital when desiring a relationship with those whose capacity to recall is, at best, compromised.

With each passing day those consigned here struggle to maintain what remains of their short-term memory or STM. AD remains the most common type of dementia and is more prevalent today than ever among seniors. Currently nearly six million elders in America are living with the disease and numbers are expected to triple by the year 2030.

AD follows a slow and insidious course of eroding the portion of our brain responsible for memory and other functions such as cognition, speech and motor skills. Some here decline quietly while pacing the halls, rarely muttering even so much as a word while others work overtime to pester and annoy staff such as with the Troll. In either case, all need continual monitoring and can no longer function freely as they once did.

Newcomers undergo the painful lesson of learning reliance. Gone are the days when they could live independently and do as they pleased. Placed here out of safety concerns and mostly by fellow family members, they're often very lonely. What they need most is daily exposure with someone willing to invest the time needed to buffer the staging process. Staff members along with fellow residents are all they will have for socializing from here on out. Each day brings new challenges as we work to meet the needs of nearly three dozen individuals who no longer possess the ability to reason or rationalize and who, at times, may not even recognize their own reflection.

Prior to their placement here, residents regressed through a series of stages. Those in the initial stages are essentially asymptomatic and show no obvious signs of having AD. Over time however, the disease slowly begins to rear its ugly head. Subtle changes begin to occur such as difficulty with balancing check books, scheduling appointments or forgetting names. Eventually lapses in STM become more frequent along with speech difficulties, loss of muscle coordination, and shuffling of feet—a hallmark of AD. Finally, the family members of those afflicted become overwhelmed and relocation to a unit becomes necessary.

Once here, the staging process continues. Without some form of regular interaction, I've witnessed residents to deteriorate more quickly to the final stages of their illness. A few residents have family or friends visit on occasion, but the majority do not; and thus, are now *socially isolated*. Finding time to connect with them while fulfilling my duties demands very strict time management and occurs mostly at the wagon while handing out meds. Late afternoon brings a whole new set of challenges and requires that we maintain a constant state of vigilance for residents attempting to flee. Working here is about being flexible in an environment which is confined and restricted.

As staff, we're called to exercise a type of emotional endurance not normally observed among today's workforce. Over the course of many years the constant repeating, reminding and redirecting can wear on you.

Many of the responsibilities here include assisting with personal care, which is often met with [at best] an apathetic response or [at worst] complete refusal. While higher functioning residents are usually open to receiving help, convincing others of the need to change their undergarment can prove to be impossible.

Changes in mood or behavior can fluctuate daily and range anywhere from being congenial and helpful to being argumentative and even combative. This day to day challenge requires that we constantly comb our unit for signs which spell trouble. Like a lit fuse on its way to a bomb, certain behaviors such as appearing anxious, fearful or labile are clear indicators of an impending meltdown. Feelings of paranoia and fear can easily overcome certain residents, especially in late afternoon. Understanding this perceived fear and being in tune to their feelings are key when entering their personal space. Without the ability to recognize their surroundings, including staff, they can quickly deteriorate emotionally and begin to act out.

Sadly, their receptive and expressive limitations often preclude them from understanding and communicating their needs. This is especially true for lower functioning residents when changes in mood seem to peak. The key to helping residents overcome these difficulties is to have well-trained staff members who possess a special knack for loving and understanding the needs of others. Staff consistency, employee cohesiveness and team building are all crucial elements when it comes to working in a setting such as ours. For some the progression is faster than others but for each is coming a day when they will be forced to face the full fury of their illness—with the only exception being death. Inexhaustible patience along with a strong willingness to serve others are a must.

In addition to problems with speech, residents eventually require total assistance with ADLs (Activities of Daily Living), feeding and escorting to and from meals. Eventually, residents must be fed and may require a special diet. These diets range from mechanical soft or textured modified to a total puree diet which means eating a meal through a straw. Also, thickened liquids may be required due to swallowing difficulties.

Those in the end stage simply refuse to eat and are found without the ability to speak, bound to a wheelchair, half asleep; a point at which the disease fully *owns* them.

A Familiar Stranger

Reflections

"We have a fall in the day area!" My portable radio sounds.

"On my way."

Our Rembrandt's day area is an open, centrally located living room where residents attend activities, work puzzles and watch television. The unit is shaped like a giant H, with the day area occupying most of the center portion. I often refer to it as the executive lounge within our gated community.

Locking the wagon, I head for my fall victim. I am suddenly confronted by Ed, who is distraught and labile. "I have to go; I have to go now! My wife! She's been waiting for over an hour!"

Knowing Ed's wife died over a year ago, I gently reassure and instruct him to have a seat until I return and reluctantly, he agrees. Ed is balding, every bit of six five and 250 pounds with not an ounce of fat.

Never would I mention to him that his wife has passed as it would destroy him emotionally, possibly place my own safety in jeopardy and serve no real purpose.

It never ceases to amaze me how someone with Alzheimer's can escape a locked unit undetected, but it happens more often than one may think. Some here like Ed who are in the early to mid-stages of the disease can converse and interact as though they have no cognitive limitations. These periods of lucidity occur more commonly in the AM hours but by early afternoon tend to wear off.

My arrival at the day area is met with the problem of crowd control in addition to assessing my fall victim whose fellow residents are attempting to help stand. Molly and Thelma each have a hand of my fallen resident, and slowly they begin helping her up.

"No!" I shout. "She may be injured!"

Along with my colleagues, we clear the onlookers and discover Joann (also known as Crack Shot) who has no injuries and simply wanted to sit on the floor. That will be about 20 minutes of paperwork…I think as I prepare to help her stand. She earned the name crack shot after winning first place in a skeet shooting contest at Northwestern during her freshmen year – 1939. Helping her up, I feel the Troll pushing her walker against my legs, pestering me again about her pills. Before I can answer her, I hear shouting coming from a doorway behind me.

"Get out! Get out!"

I hurry only to discover Esther who's very agitated about a stranger in her room. Once again, she's failed to recognize her own reflection and is now distressed about the foreigner standing before her. Bizarre but true.

Aides, Laura and Coleen help to reassure and relocate her to the day area while I assist Mildred; who cannot remember her name and is beginning to escalate. Concurrent with this, several other residents begin to quarrel over the TV remote, and a physical confrontation ensues. Amidst the mayhem, I faintly hear a request on the overhead for me to answer a phone call from a physician who's been placed on hold. En route to the call, I help to quell the fisticuffs and quickly insert the Johnny Mathis "Chances Are" CD into our boom box.

Now late afternoon, the sun downing hour is in full swing. A condition used to describe a noticeable change in mood and behavior, sun downing is characterized by a willingness to wander, increased confusion, anxiety and agitation. Although sun downing is frequently associated with Alzheimer's, it doesn't always occur among those diagnosed with AD. Over the years however I've discovered that those afflicted with AD who initially show no tendency to sun down, do appear to be at an increased risk for developing it down the road.

The Rembrandt is becoming increasingly busy today, and emotions are heightened. At times, you can feel the tension in the air. I refer to the unit as being "hot" when it gets to this point and know that at any moment, things could go south. Today's chaos is par for the course, and with employee turnover as bad as it's been, I am growing more discouraged than ever. I suspect this to be the norm for many memory units today.

The noise level is noticeably louder and my stress has gone up a notch. The Troll is now yelling at me about her pills and I can smell that's she's muddy. Attempts to contract or redirect her is futile as she only hears what she wants while shouting at me all the louder. Dialing the doctor, I radio to the aides that the Troll needs to be changed. My staff acknowledges me but at the moment they're overwhelmed and following my call with Dr. Feel-good, I toilet the Troll.

Continuing with my medication pass, I look up to see the never-ending daily procession of wheelchairs and walkers heading to the dining room. I offer to help push wheelchairs before resuming my duties as today's portable pill provider.

After relocating my wagon from the far end of the center hall, I notice Lucille alone on the sofa in our day area dressed in her salmon Capri's and white pullover sweater. She has a petite frame with long thinning snow white hair and beautiful bright green eyes. At ninety years young, she's absolutely adorable and is usually Chatty Cathy during the day. She's possesses a noticeable look of worry while clinging tightly to her teddy bear, Alfie. I can tell she's beginning to sun down as she commonly does at this time and will no doubt be looking for her parents and eventually the exit.

Not sure of her surroundings, she'll soon require individual attention to quell her anxiety. I invite her to assist with filling Dixie cups with water, but receive no reply. Initially, she only stares at me while maintaining her look of fright. Like a young girl, she doesn't want to be caught looking at me and proceeds to quickly look down each time I glance her way. Continuing to multitask, I do my best to return her a warm smile but my efforts are of little value.

When Lucille and others sun down, they change in a very distinctive way. In addition to their anxiety, fear and mistrust, some develop a strong eagerness to leave the unit. For others, if their emotional needs aren't promptly addressed, they'll become verbally violent and insist that we allow them to leave. And sadly, some like Lucille, internalize their anxiety by suffering quietly before emotionally imploding.

She is lost and her need to feel safe and secure is greater than ever. Sensing her emotional instability, I stop dispensing and take a moment to reassure her with a gentle hug. I offer her an anti-anxiety medication, but she declines. Cautiously, she allows me to escort her to the dining room but only after extensive coaxing. As we begin to walk, I'm reminded of my role as a caregiver in fulfilling our residents' needs. She squeezes my hand with the force necessary to open a new jar of pickles while maintaining her tight hold on Alfie. It warms my heart to know that for the moment she feels protected and her beautiful smile is reminder enough that I *know* I'm right where I should be.

To love others is important, but equally important is to be loved *by* others. A lesson on how to understand love as a verb; this is what we do.

Communication here is everything. Timely recognition and proper engagement are essential to each encounter, and efficacious results can sometimes seem impossible. Verbal prompting and reassurance aren't always enough and as competent caregivers we must possess the ability to clearly communicate without the use of speech.

Effective communication is a two-way street, and most here are driving a Model-T on a dirt road. This is most challenging as I'm having to operate more like a high-speed train to complete my tasks on time. Occasionally, a resident will arrive at the wagon emotionally distraught because they cannot pronounce the words they desperately want to say. With a pen and paper, I spell out each letter before finding the words to construct sentences. For a moment, it's all smiles as we find the words before repeating the same sentence over several times.

Knowing how to say "please allow me to help you" without the use of words is what we specialize in. Whistling is one way to communicate without the use of speech. Many of our residents will usually whistle along to favorites such as <u>Bridge over River Kwai</u> march or <u>Singing in the Rain.</u> This is a great way to break the ice with a resident who is in no mood to contract with staff.

Touch is also a powerful tool and is no doubt the key to providing a certain quality of care. Residents who can no longer verbalize their needs frequently require a loving touch to help calm their fears. Therapeutic touch commonly occurs when close interaction is needed, such as my brief escort with Lucille or when assisting with personal care duties; dressing, bathing or toileting.

At times, residents can react negatively to touch and we must be extra cautious when entering their personal space. This is especially true of residents who may be confused, irritable and on the verge of acting out. It's imperative that we recognize certain telltale behaviors before a situation develops. Working understaffed rarely allows for us to meet these needs and sadly some residents go unattended.

We do our best to complete our tasks while monitoring the unit but are sometimes overcome when multiple residents suddenly need emotional support. This is when my job gets tough. On occasion and without warning, numerous residents will crowd in on me at once, each insisting that they be attended to first. I'll never forget a unique situation I experienced years ago, while at the wagon.

Late one afternoon while handing out meds, several residents began yelling at each other over who was first in line when suddenly I abruptly stopped dispensing, stood straight, placed my hand on my heart and began reciting the Pledge of Allegiance. "I…pledge of allegiance to the flag …" very slowly each joined in and at the completion of "with liberty and justice for all."...they all were standing straight, with hands on hearts in total silence. It was like a scene from a Broadway play. I realized I'd better do something fast to avoid a reoccurrence, so I radioed for help and began to sing..."Show me the way to go home...I'm tired and I want to go to bed." Once again, each participant slowly joined in and as the *sing-a-long* ended, additional staff arrived (also singing) and escorted the performers to each of their apartments.

All medications were made available for administration as I discovered a new way to complete my tasks while keeping the peace on the unit. Also, I made handheld American flags available which we hold high on occasion when singing such favorites as our National Anthem and The Battle Hymn of the Republic, when things get heated.

Usually we can help to reorient sun downers by directing their thought process, but having things run smoothly requires more than meets the eye. Our priority is to see to their safety while providing a comfortable living environment which sometimes calls for us to abandon our comfort zones and act as entertainers.

Additionally, we are charged with the responsibility of making sure our residents feel loved—like family.

From here on out, this is their home and it's up to us to make the most of it. A unique type of worker commitment along with employers who genuinely value their staff are needed if we are to meet the needs of those afflicted with this terrible disease. Today, this combination is rarely found despite an ever-growing need for its demand.

Helping to redirect dozens of seniors who are confused and perhaps agitated can prove to be harder than one may think. It's imperative that we keep our mental radar going by remaining acutely aware of our surroundings. Certain locations such as the dining room are now crowded and tempers can easily flare. Anti-agitation medications are effective only if administered prior to residents beginning to escalate, which is not always so obvious.

Situational awareness is a huge part of keeping the peace here and requires us to remain vigilant. A physical confrontation can erupt without notice resulting in harm to both residents and staff. If I sense a situation might be brewing, I immediately intervene and relocate residents to separate locations. Knowing how to recognize body language is key to early intervention and avoiding what could become an all-out confrontation.

Despite having worked here for nearly a decade, I

still struggle to understand why certain residents escalate rapidly and who may be highly resistive to being redirected. Some here can become easily agitated if put into an environment of too much stimulus. They can quickly become overwhelmed if placed into a loud or crowded environment. Blaring noises, bright lights, or being touched unexpectedly are just a few triggers that act to escalate certain residents. Even dressing in colorful clothing such as Hawaiian shirts can sometimes elicit a negative response.

For years, I've worked on improving how to effectively interact with residents who respond or react unexpectedly to their surroundings. I've gotten better, but on occasion I am made aware of how much I don't know. Learning how to interpret body language is crucial. We once had a resident (Carol) who never spoke. To this day, I'm not sure if she suffered from a condition known as expressive aphasia (an ailment in which one cannot speak, usually due to a stroke) or whether she merely chose not to speak. No attempt from either myself or my team members ever resulted in her muttering so much as a word. She constantly paced the halls and on occasion would attempt to remove the fire extinguisher from its location behind a glass door.

Critical thinking helped us to realize that she may

just have soreness, most likely due to arthritic joint discomfort. After administering an extra strength pain reliever, her pacing slowed, and she no longer showed interest in the fire extinguisher. We concluded she was no longer able to verbalize her needs and when her hurting became unbearable, she acted out; A lesson on the importance of being proactive with critical thought.

Engaging angry residents are certainly not without challenges and should I fail to pick up on what is understood to be a red flag, my job becomes even more difficult. If a resident is in the beginning stages of escalation, my responsibility is to find a way of communicating with them before they begin to act out. If they allow me into their personal space when I approach them, I'm on the road to peace; if not, I have my work cut out for me. Discovering ways to connect with them includes not only departing my comfort zone but sometimes calls for me to act downright silly. If residents aren't entertained, fellow staff members usually are.

Sometimes I'll sing or ask for a dance in an effort to contract with them when all else fails. I've discovered this approach to be quite effective when separating residents who may be arguing or residents who refuse to change their clothes. Again, it's more of my stand-up comedy routine I do and when I get at least one to trust me, others will usually follow. However ridiculous and unorthodox my behavior may be, it speaks to them in a language they still understand, the language of laughter. A lesson on how to not take life—too seriously.

Each day, we can never be sure of how our residents may choose to interact with others. At times, they can be quite entertaining and will not hesitate to tell you what they are thinking. Occasionally, they'll be sexually inappropriate, causing the staff to blush. We once had a lady who would walk the halls repeating,

"Young at heart...other parts slightly older."

As staff members, we're often caught off guard by certain residents' comments and can't help but laugh. The former radio and TV personality Art Linkletter was known to frequently visit retirement centers such as ours. Years ago, during a stopover at a local rest home, he paused briefly to ask a lady in a wheelchair, "Do you know who I am?" "No, she replied. "But if you ask the nurse at the front desk, she'll tell you."

After completing my early med pass, I roll the wagon back to the office and notice Ed stuttering in broken conversation with Paula and Hazel. Despite having three watches on her left wrist, Hazel has spent much of the afternoon asking others what time it is. She's apparently determined that either Ed or Paula must know the answer and proceeds to sheepishly interrogate them. The Troll waddles by with Mr. Robinson in tow.

"It's dinner time…that's what time it is." She blurts.

So engrossed in their discussion, they are oblivious to the eight-foot grandfather clock (Captain Kangaroo) opposite them gonging away. Paula's socks are cute; one red and one blue. So much of working here is simply learning to roll with the punches.

Laura approaches and we direct them to the dining room. Once seated, I administer Ed a mild sedative while Laura synchronizes Hazel's watches. We do a head count to ensure everyone made it to dinner as kitchen personnel enter with tonight's entrée.

"What is that?" Laura asks.

"Yesterday's leftovers." answers a kitchen worker who looks to be no older than twelve.

"Looks like, chicken and…waffles?" Laura comments with a look of disbelief.

After restocking my wagon, I'm needing to do blood-sugar testing for one resident over in the Van Gogh, the assisted living area of our complex. It is now five o' clock and I'm beginning to wonder where my admission is.

I take a moment to grab what's left of the coffee before heading back to my office. Once there, I discover only two physicians' orders and one lab result to fax. Not bad for a Friday…I think while pondering to make more coffee. Next I review our newcomer's paperwork. His name is Steve and he's carried a diagnosis of dementia for some time. His profile describes him as pleasantly confused and like others here is undergoing relocation for safety concerns due to his eagerness to wander from home.

Admissions are time-consuming but also very interesting as I learn essentially an individual's life history while completing my intake questionnaire. Frequently I receive detailed admission data directly from those relocating to the Van Gogh whereas admissions to the Rembrandt require a family member's input. Remarkably, some admitted to the Van Gogh maintain very sharp memories despite being well into their eighties and even nineties!

I'm privileged with learning where they were born, lived, worked, went to school, raised their families, etc. My duties include collecting health history information which I often find fascinating. I love to ask older ones if they knew their grandparents. It's like taking a trip back in time to hear what people have experienced over the course of their lives and how it's shaped their opinion of our world today. I look forward to meeting Steve and getting to know as much as I can about him but for now, I'm off to the AL side.

Exiting my office, the doorbell sounds. Visitors are provided this feature at the entrance to alert staff when they arrive. After disarming the lock feature, I invite in Fred, Betty's husband. He's just arrived from the hospital and provides me an update.

"Hey Fred, how is she doing?"

"Better, she's doing better. They said her heart appears normal and there is even a chance that she'll come back tonight. So …what exactly happened again?"

I explained in detail the fiasco as we walked to her room. He wants to pick up a sweater, hairbrush and lipstick.

"I've noticed over these last several weeks that she's just not the same." He says, removing a sweater from its hanger. "She's more confused and just seems…well…out of it. Last week she didn't even know who I was. Have *you* noticed any difference?"

"Well, yes I have. She has staged over these past few weeks. She's very happy though. She often keeps me occupied while I pass meds and I enjoy being with her. I know it must be hard for you to see her this way." I give a gentle pat to his sleeve. This is one of the very hard times when loved ones watch their spouses progressively get worse.

"Well...that's the disease I guess. I'll call if they decide to admit her."

"Okay, that sounds good, thanks Fred."

Quietly, we exit the unit. Slowly, he entered the elevator and we said goodnight.

Fred is doing his best to understand what occurred today but also to accept what changes Betty has recently undergone. Aside from today's incident, Betty's inability to recognize him earlier in the week has dealt him a powerful emotional blow. I can tell he is doing his best to cope. Before getting on my way, I make myself a note to call him if I don't hear from him tonight. I feel his pain.

Welcome to Assisted Living,
we hope you enjoy your stay
For help just pull your bed call cord,
and staff is on the way
We shop and mop and adjust your clock
at least two times a year
On Friday's we have happy hour,
with whiskey wine and beer
We cook and clean and wash your jeans,
once or twice a week,
Make your bed and give you meds,
even help you take a leak

Calmer Waters

Working in the Van Gogh doesn't require a level of awareness such as that needed in the Rembrandt. In a sense, I'm allowed to let my guard down—a little. It's usually much less stressful out here, and passing meds can be a piece of cake. The Van Gogh comprises eighty individual apartments which surround the Rembrandt, in a shape similar to that of the pentagon. A slight scent of potpourri permeates the air and my keys are all I hear at this time of day. The dated hallways are strangely reminiscent of those seen in <u>The Shining</u>. I realized this late one evening after I was hired to work overnights. The following morning, I put in a request to work days.

Every hallway is identical in appearance and can easily challenge a newcomer's sense of direction. It's a not-so-fun house of mirrors for some of our new admits. They struggle to navigate this never-ending maze of corridors and we frequently reorient lost souls. An abundance of patience is required as any reminders are rarely retained beyond the next scheduled meal. This can go on for weeks following an admission and reoccurs as their memory fails.

These halls house one unmistakable reality—loneliness. The longer I'm here, the more I sense its depressive presence. Each room I walk past is home to at least one occupant in the final chapter of life. Stop in to say hi and you'll likely become a new best friend while viewing an endless assortment of family photos.

Additional photos of grandchildren, great-grandchildren and extended family members often dominate the apartment. Also, you may be asked to perform a small task such as replacing the batteries of a TV remote, adjusting the digital clock on a microwave, or threading an embroidery needle. Prior to entering certain apartments, I have actually asked a fellow staff member to call me on the radio shortly after I enter. This is done in an effort to rescue me from a resident who refuses to allow any visitor to leave.

Fortunately, some are a joy to visit. Gwen is one such resident and as a retired nurse she always brightens my day. She's "Dionne Warwick" in every way except only older and is the furthest thing from being possessive or self-absorbed. Around here, she is a rarity. Tapping on her door, I discover she's out. I feel disappointment and tell myself that I'll stop by later—wishful thinking.

I'd give anything to have her complexion when I get older but seriously doubt that possibility as I don't possess that skin now. She looks amazing for her age of eighty-nine!

As a supervisor, I often float, which means I'm required to cover both the Rembrandt and the Van Gogh. On occasion, another nurse may be scheduled, but doesn't function as a charge nurse. I gladly welcome another nurse on board as it provides me a much-needed break from having to cover so much ground. Tonight, however I'm the only nurse supervisor, making me responsible for all residents. I fear being pulled away from The Rembrandt for too long as I may pay a price when I return.

Working with a little stress keeps me on my toes. If not continually faced with situations requiring critical thought and intervention, I'll lose my edge and let down my guard. This could result in injury or harm to residents or staff and destroy any trust I've worked to develop over the years.

Checking the volume on my portable radio, I briskly head for the central nurse's station. As usual it's buzzing with staff members trying to stay out of each other's way.

"We've got a staff meeting at five o' clock," I hear as I enter.

Seated at the computer is Sherri, otherwise known as Nurse Suck Up. As one of the four nurses on staff, she usually works NOC's [over nights] and oversees scheduling monthly staff meetings. Dressed in colorful scrubs, she appears warmer than she really is. Her half smile is no exaggeration and often she's downright rude.

"Oh great…and how are you today?" I respond sarcastically contorting the same semi smile.

The phone rings, and she answers it. Wonderful I think, now maybe I can get out of here without having to talk to her. The caller ID reads "Physicians Associates" so I eavesdrop to see which resident it pertains to. Sherri is placed on hold and proceeds to tap her fingers on the counter while staring at me. I never can figure out why she always stares at me!

With today's meeting making my schedule even tighter, I immediately assemble Sam's blood-sugar test kit and head for his room. I return only moments later having discovered he's not there. As I disassemble the test kit, Sherri informs me that he's at therapy and should be back shortly. That witch…I say to myself. She could have told me that as I was assembling the kit instead of just staring at me. This is what aggravates me and others about Sherri. A coworker once commented "In kindergarten she never got her box checked, the one labeled works well with others." At times, I have to agree!

Soon I'm able to clear two phone messages and transcribe an order before making my first rounds, starting again with Sam. Returning to his room, I discover him to be resting in his E-Z chair sipping a tall glass of ice water. I can tell he's tired and thirsty following his half-hour physical therapy session. He was admitted to us several months back, and requires blood-sugar monitoring at least four times daily but rarely requires insulin. His appearance is that of worn leather complemented by what's left of his thinning auburn rug. His looks are age appropriate with features like the late great Johnny Cash.

"Working hard tonight?" he bellows.

"As always."

"Whenever you have time, I sure would like to finish going through that photo album with you."

"How about tonight after eight?" I ask.

"That would be great…remind me, though…seems lately my minds been AWOL." he responds creasing a smile.

Sam is a WWII navy veteran who in 1944 was left

adrift in the Philippine Sea when his destroyer mine sweeper sunk out from under him after being struck by the Japanese. His history is truly amazing; and I could easily spend hours talking with him over photo albums. Veterans on campus are a dying breed of the grandest generation. Without a doubt, Tom Brokaw was spot on when he helped to convey the message that Sam's generation is the greatest we may ever know.

"Well, your sugar looks great…no insulin for now," I say applying a small Band Aid to his index finger. "I'll see you at eight."

He gives a gentle salute.

Exiting is always the same. I sense his disappointment and then my guilty alarm goes off. The large invisible sign over his door has only gotten larger, *PLEASE DON'T GO…YET!* Sam is terribly lonely and my heart aches for him. He yearns for someone to sit and listen to him but with my schedule, I'm forced to ignore what now is his greatest need—companionship; An awkward lesson on failing to meet the emotional needs of another senior who now feels shelved. We both feel pain.

After departing, I quickly suppress my sorrows about another forgotten elder and head to the clinic; an office just up the hall. As usual, I discover it to be cramped and bustling with fellow staff. Nurses' aides, social workers, medication technicians and therapist are all competing for space in what amounts to be an over-sized broom closet. I find at least an hour's worth of orders to process along with multiple phone messages and—a last glazed doughnut. Hmmm...decisions decisions.

After gathering what napkins and paperwork I need, I head back to the central nurse's station. Prior to my arrival, I stop in to say hi and assess Delores. She's a *fossil*. In three weeks, she'll be 108 years young and yet remains alert and oriented on most days.

Recently she acquired her second hearing aid and I can't say it's made a great deal of difference. The day she was fitted I remember inquiring about the brand she'd purchased as other residents are forever asking what make of hearing aid I feel is best. I'll never forget our conversation.

"What kind is it?"

"WHAT?" she replied.

"WHAT KIND IS IT?"

Looking down at her watch she replied..."It's four fifteen."

I just smiled...and mouthed thank you.

Arriving at her apartment, things are as I expected. As usual she's reading her large print edition of <u>Readers</u>

<u>Digest</u> while relaxing in her recliner. Knocking loudly on her door, I yell;

"Good afternoon, I'm looking for a friendly young lady by the name of Delores."

"Well, I think she's still friendly but she sure ain't young." she creaked while laughing.

Everybody loves this lady. She's a hoot!

"How are you doing? I don't get to see you much anymore." she says while attempting to sit up.

"I know...I mostly work in the Rembrandt on nights when I have help. The decision to staff only one nurse for both the Rembrandt and Van Gogh five days a week doesn't allow me to see you as much. How are you feeling? I see your ankles aren't doing so great."

"Oh, I'm doing okay...I just can't stop eating those nuts and I know they're full of salt."

Delores, at times, has swollen ankles; a condition known as *edema*. The term refers to excess fluids somewhere in the body and can be caused by any number of reasons. As for Delores, her heart has weakened with age and cannot provide the circulation required to remove this excess fluid. The greatest danger for her is fluid possibly backing up into her lungs—causing pneumonia.

Most physicians will usually prescribe a water pill known as a diuretic. The aspirin-sized tablet acts to draw fluids out of the body by increasing urination, sort of like caffeine. Looking up at me with her Coke bottle glasses and big smile, she appears happy, which is no doubt why she's lived to such a ripe old age. Most of those I care for simply don't laugh enough. I take a minute to listen to her lungs and remind her to prop her feet up whenever she's able.

"Other than your ankles it looks like you're doing pretty good…no pain?"

"None at all." Her smile is priceless! Holding hands, I check her pulse and tell her I'll try to stop in more often. Exiting, I notice a calendar full of unreadable handwritten reminders of activities and appointments. Honestly, I hope to live to be half her age.

Once back at the central nurse's station, I attempt to reach her great, great, grandson. Family notification is a must for any resident who experiences a change in labs, orders or conditions. Unable to reach him, I leave a message and write myself a sticky note to follow up. Next, I'm able to transcribe several orders from the clinic and return a phone call before charting. Entering my desk area, I'm greeted by Monique. She is a long-time employee here and possesses a vast amount of experience in working with senior citizens. Friendly and full of energy; her long black hair glistens against her olive skin.

I've often wondered how old she is but never could find the courage to ask her. She relocated here from Italy decades ago and since then has been employed in the healthcare field in one capacity or another.

She is our senior medical assistant and works in the capacity of medication technician. She, and others are responsible for medication administration to well over one hundred residents. Looking at the employee work schedule, she comments with a sigh,

"Looks like Jo Ann won't be coming in again today."

"Yeah" I reach for Sam's chart to document his blood sugar. "Her last chemotherapy was two days ago, and her radiation treatments begin October first."

Monique and Joann have been friends for nearly twenty years and are both breast cancer survivors.

"Me and some of the others here got her a gift basket and this card. When you get a chance, can you please sign it?" She says trying her best to appear hopeful.

"Absolutely…you okay?" I ask.

"I'm not so sure she's going to make it this time." She fights to hold back her tears.

I take hold of her hands. "You're the best friend Joann could have ever asked for; you've never let her down." Looking into her soft dark eyes, I feel her concern.

"Thanks," she whispers. "But I can tell she just doesn't want to live anymore I've been there, I know."

"Did she tell you that?"

"No, no, I can just tell."

Handing her a tissue I tell her if she needs any time off—that it's fine. "She's a strong lady." I add.

"She sure is. I'm going to see her tomorrow morning," she says wiping her eyes, regaining her composure.

"Well good, if she's up for anybody else to visit, I'd sure like to."

"Oh no!" she responds raising her hand. "I think I'm pushing it by going over there myself, but I know she needs me."

"Okay, can I donate to the gift basket?"

"No no no!" she insists. "We've got it covered. If you could just run this card back to the Rembrandt so the others could sign it that would be great."

"No problem." I slowly secure it to my clipboard. Exiting the office, I do my best to reassure her with a warm hug. "She's going to be fine, we're all praying for her."

"I know," she responds with a warm smile.

"We've got to go to that stupid meeting now, you ready?" I ask.

"Yea, as ready as I'll ever be."

Marionettes

Monthly meetings are for the most part a big waste of time. Despite being mandatory, they're often cancelled at the last minute. When we do meet, the *real* issue is never addressed or resolved—staffing numbers! An open house earlier in the week results in an abundance of chairs scattered about the conference room and we're all afforded a rare opportunity to sit. Once seated, we circulate a sign-in sheet so management will pay us for attending, but only because state law requires it. Our corporate offices would assign the housekeeping and dietary staff to administer medications and give flu vaccines if regulations allowed. Margin of profit is *all* that matters.

In charge of the meeting is Marie, our director of Nurses or DON. Most would say she's DONe as she possesses little patience and has been here too long. Also present is our Senior Health Administrator, Carol. One look at Carol will lead you to think; please do something with your hair! People have asked her if she's related to

Phyllis Diller. Her plus-sized frame dominates the meeting and I've often felt a large Cuban cigar would nicely complete her. Bossy and tyrannical, Carol looks down on those around her as being less than her. Cold and indifferent to the needs of both residents and staff; above all the aides, Carol is the captain of her ship and will not hesitate to remind those under her of who's in charge.

She's made many a worker walk the plank, some deservedly so, but also as a show of force. Her favorite is requiring new hires sign a *no compete clause.* The document forbids employees from working private duty for any competitors in the area should they decide to resign; thereby forcing workers to either relocate or pursue a different line of work altogether. All who labor here are convinced that one day, she'll get what she has coming to her.

Both she and Marie are merely *marionettes* to the corporate offices and function as they're told, to increase profits! I could never have their jobs as I'm far too outspoken not to mention that I deeply care about our residents and my co-workers. Sounding like a "Wheels on the Bus" ad for the American Heart Association, Carol opens the meeting with an unexpected bit of news.

"It has been brought to our attention that someone has defaced company property."

"What happened?" A whisper sounds with curious looks.

"Apparently during the open house, someone altered the Please Don't Feed the Squirrels sign located at the main entrance to read...Please don't feed the *employees*!"

Muffled laughter erupts which only fuels Carol's anger.

"Oh, you think this is funny, well this is no joking matter and we *will* find out who did this. We have cameras everywhere and when I discover who it is...they'll be prosecuted!"

Suddenly, pin drop silence is broken by the sound of a loud swallow. With nothing said, we are on to addressing other important issues such as how to properly answer the telephone along with where and when it's appropriate to use the restroom. Next management opens the floor to questions, comments or concerns. Are you kidding me?...I think, struggling to appear interested.

The response initially of those in attendance is one of total indifference. Their body language speaks volumes as most have their head down in total discouragement. They know things will never change. The topic of hiring adequate help isn't even brought up anymore.

Seated across from me is Tina. She's cool. She's our

seven am - three pm weekday nurse in the Rembrandt. Years ago, we met while attending nursing school at the local college here in our town of East Maple. In training, we became good friends and over the years have grown even closer. Just prior to completing her preceptorship, (a two-week period of on the job training for nurses) she accepted a position here to work nights after graduation. Approximately one year later I applied and started working nights also. Since then we've both switched to a saner schedule.

Seated to my left is Suck up, and opposite her is a new face whose name tag reads *Robin.* Another new hire that's joined the ranks of healthcare galley rower I think while searching my scrubs for a pen. Despite wearing a long sleeve turtleneck sweater, he is unable to cover all his graffiti. Built like a linebacker, he has a noticeable presence.

Perhaps a recent graduate from the correctional school for nursing; or who knows maybe the body piercing college of medicine. A closer look reveals horned-rimmed specs, a spotless shave and a perfectly cropped flat top complete with rat tail. Carol extends him a warm welcome and the opportunity to introduce himself.

"Hi, I'm Robin...It's good to be here."

He speaks with a near whisper, and we all suddenly

lean in. I can tell Carol and Marie are perplexed. They expect him to say more, but he only smiles and nods. We each introduce ourselves and welcome him onboard.

Soon Carol assigns Robin to shadow with Tina and me on alternating schedules for two weeks to acclimate him to the Rembrandt. I remember when I was hired and how awkward I felt.

Robin is struggling to fit in. Despite being welcomed by fellow workers, our newcomer remains quiet—too quiet, almost to the point of suspicion.

He'll never last. He's *way* too passive. He is going to have to learn assertiveness the hard way. Wait till he has to deal with the Troll and the unit begins to boil over. It will prove his leadership abilities and like all the others, he'll be gone in a week or two.

Reaching for the sign-in sheet from Carol, I notice Tina smirking. She's caught me staring at Robin and I'm convinced she knows who changed that sign at the entrance. Monique and the others are pretending to appear attentive while fiddling with their phones. Most of what is covered regarding bathroom privileges, dress code and telephone etiquette is painfully boring and is no doubt tuned out by those in attendance.

Oh my, I think, what fun we're having. Also present

are aides Laura and Coleen. Both are high school students looking to get into the nursing program after graduation. Hired to work in the Van Gogh, neither has set foot in the assisted living due to staff shortages in the Rembrandt.

I've proudly earned the nickname ADHD, as I talk too fast and struggle with staying on task. Some say it's only ADD, but I say I'm normal. What is normal anyway? Tina once told me normal is only a setting on the washing machine and not to worry.

Seated at the far end of the table is Jane. She is our day nurse in Van Gogh during the week and every other weekend. With striking facial features, silky long blond hair and tall slender build she looks more like a runway super model. Over the years, I've worked with all kinds of people of diverse backgrounds, but never with someone like Jane. We all have strengths and weaknesses and Jane is certainly no exception. She works very well with the elder population but demonstrates little if no patience with others, especially the support staff. She's the queen of amphetamine. Day to day, it's strictly conjecture as to what her mood will be. I'm guessing that she's on more meds than most who live here.

Fellow workers usually avoid her altogether as they don't want to *deal* with her attitude. The aides tend to walk on egg shells around her to avoid any type of confrontation.

She's been here nearly eighteen years and the staff wonders why she just doesn't retire. Divorced twice with no children, she acquired two rental properties as part of her latest break up and is rumored to be somewhat of a slum lord. She most likely wouldn't know what to do with herself if she did retire, so like Marie, she's hanging on to the bitter end.

"We need volunteers to go through the storage closets and dispose of expired medications, starting in the Rembrandt. Fines for being in possession of expired medications are $100 per pill. Overnights have not had time and state inspectors are due here any day. Also, we need to prepare for our annual corporate review, any takers?" Carol barks out while shuffling papers.

Silence.

"How about you two?" Marie says, pointing at me and Robin.

"Sure, we can do that." I respond with a quick glance at Robin. I'd like to stare but can't.

Before we can say another word, a desperation call rings out in stereo from our radios.

"Nurse needed in the Rembrandt, stat!"

I grab my portable radio; but before I can leave,

Carol instructs Robin to accompany me and together we dart. Running toward the Rembrandt is not uncommon for me and will occur at least twice a shift. Usually it's a fall, a fight or possible elopement. Approaching the unit, we're met with a high-pitched tone of the door alarm. The siren sounds whenever the door crossbar is touched, even slightly, thus indicating an unauthorized attempt to exit the unit.

Entering, we are confronted by Ed who, once again, is insistent on going to meet his wife. My first efforts at redirecting him while resetting the keypad to silence the alarm are ill effective and he is becoming increasingly angry and hostile. Concurrent with this I notice a local pharmacy courier opposite the door also wanting into the unit. I motion to her to hold on and she acknowledges with an impatient look. This situation has always been a challenge for us as Ed is a flight risk. Fearing he'll make a break for it, Robin and I stand our ground. Suddenly, Robin has become a much-needed layer of protection and I feel slightly guilty for doubting him.

"Ed...please tell me how I can help you."

"Let me out of here!" he shouts with a clinched fist.

Uh oh, it's show time, I think as all eyes are now on me. Another lesson on tough love.

"Ed, please tell me where she is and we will go." On

the outside I appear cool as a cucumber while on the inside I'm scared to death. Struggling with every ounce of self-control, I'm barely able to keep from shaking and hyperventilating.

"Tell you where she is? You tell me! You have all the answers!" he shouts.

Knowing we're at a stalemate, I offer to help in a way which will act to deescalate him.

"Before we go, you will need to take your medication." My wimpy attempt at being authoritative isn't working. "Remember what your wife said about taking your meds? Ed, how would it be if you wait here for me...please...and after you take your pills, we will go. Fair enough?"

His stare remains fixated on Robin. Slowly, his expression turned from one of panic and anger to look of sorrowful vacancy and his eyes began to moisten. Carefully, I extended my hand before entering his personal space.

"It's okay, Ed. We'll take care of you." I whispered.

Unsure of what to do, he could only stand frozen, cornered at the entrance in silence, while looking back at us—lost. I could sense the uneasiness of my coworkers as we waited. Now was my chance to demonstrate to Ed and the others that no matter how difficult working here can be, love always wins. Cautiously, I moved to embrace him when I hear a loud gasp. His hug felt like a hydraulic press and clearly communicated to me and my staff, I'm sorry. Many placed into memory care are uniquely affected in that they simply cannot process the need to be behind locked doors. Any explanation may need to be repeated dozens of times over the course of weeks and possibly months; and some like Ed lose control before lashing out.

I often think of how emotionally invested I've become over the years with certain residents and of all the heartfelt dividends to come my way, this was perhaps the most memorable. Ed demonstrated his remorse by choosing to squeeze me. It remains the deepest emotion I've ever been shown.

With Robin's help, I'm able to slowly escort him back to his table along with a small crowd that has congregated including the Troll.

"What time you gonna give me my meds?" She blurts at Robin.

Robin looked at me, not knowing exactly what to say.

"You'll get your meds at seven o'clock." I answer.

She maintains her curious stare at Robin while asking about Ed.

"He gonna be okay?" She asks.

"Yes, he'll be fine." I said with a wink and much to my chagrin, she actually winked back.

Redirecting a resident on the verge of becoming violent is a delicate issue. Although I've improved somewhat at this fine art, I realize I've still got a lot to learn. Knowing what to do is often not as important as knowing what NOT to do! One thing would be to not engage him in a way that causes further escalation such as yelling or reacting angrily. Being assertive with just the right amount of compassion is a kind of double edged sword. Knowing how to wield that sword with authority is something which only comes with time.

If not handled correctly, tonight's encounter could have easily lead to a Baker Act which starts with placing him in restraints, calling the police and transporting him to the nearest hospital with a psych unit.

Being relocated while in a fit of rage is perhaps the worst thing for someone suffering from AD as they will only continue to act out due to their inability to recognize anything. Should this occur, what usually results are the administration of stronger anti-agitation medications, which act to snow the individual. Knowing this, it's imperative that I deal with all behavioral issues in a way that allows my residents to remain here if possible.

As supervisor, I'm faced with doing what is best for those who have behavioral issues while also seeing to the safety of all parties. Understandably, this is another reason why my job carries an unusual high burnout rate and honestly, I'm amazed I've lasted this long.

Today went much easier than previous confrontations with Ed. He's never been escorted out—yet. I keep telling myself it's coming. I'm certainly no expert and sometimes find myself working purely on instinct. Many spouses have undergone the horrors of witnessing their partner escalate before having to dial 911. A resident can escalate rapidly and extreme caution must be exercised when attempting to redirect him/her.

Prevention is everything. It is here I feel that I failed Ed by not prioritizing my duties when I became focused on the fall in the day area. I should have gotten a sedative in him earlier and assigned an aide to monitor him concurrent with my being pulled away to the fall. Additional workers and delegation of duties may have avoided this whole scenario.

Management will always ask if we've tried to snow problem residents to quell their behavior. This should NOT be the answer to addressing behavioral concerns but is how managers choose to get around inadequately staffing our unit. Nearly all social interactive problems can easily be avoided with proper staffing. The following behaviors can occur at any hour but are most commonly observed during afternoon while sun downing is at its peak. Typical sun downing behaviors include:

- Pacing
- Attempting to speak rapidly
- Frequent arguing
- Acting out
- Fixating on finances
- Possessing a deer in the head lights look
- Packing a suitcase
- Asking where their car is
- Crying

All the fore-mentioned behaviors are common here and are all intended to convey a message, regardless of the actual behavior. Depending on the level of escalation, anger or hostility, most situations can be quickly defused using proper engagement. We teach our staff the following: always be on the lookout for telltale signs; and if ever they should encounter a resident escalating, immediately call for a nurse along with additional help while maintaining personal safety.

With Ed, the louder he became, the more softly I

spoke while positioning myself at a safe distance. I allowed him to feel less threatened while enabling him the freedom to vent his anger. Also, my tone of voice and facial expressions demonstrated that I genuinely wanted to help him by asking him how "I" can help "you." This conveyed that what he said was important and that his input mattered.

Convincing a resident in a state of rage to surrender is a tremendous challenge. As for Ed, his speech difficulties precluded him from telling me what he was thinking and; more important, feeling; which in turn fueled his anger. Fearing him becoming violent, I offered a solution that benefitted both of us; I mentioned "your wife;" which became the turning point of our encounter.

Agreeing to take him off the unit was not a bluff and I would have personally escorted him myself as I've done countless times. My only condition being that he demonstrates consistent appropriate behavior prior to our leaving. Moreover, I knew this would not be necessary as Ed does not maintain essentially any STM and often cannot recollect anything beyond several seconds. To my advantage, those who suffer from this terrible illness often cannot remember that they forgot. This is a double-edged sword because what can work for me today can work against me tomorrow.

All behavior we are taught is the result of legitimate unmet needs; and Ed needed to meet his wife. More importantly, his anger was merely a symptom of a much deeper issue—a loss of independence. As with all of us when we begin to grow into our senior years, we will undergo the slow and painful lesson of losing our independence in some form or another. It's not just our sight, hearing, hair or car keys we lose; for some it will also be our mind. Allowing Ed to participate in the decision-making process using questions communicated to him that his input mattered, thus allowing him to exercise what cognitive independence he still has. In other words, he wasn't merely just being told what to do. Indirectly, I asked his permission when I stated "How would it be if...?" This allowed him to feel in control, which further deescalated the encounter.

Being entrusted with the safety of both residents and employees is a tremendous responsibility and privilege for me. All stressful encounters are unique and must be treated as such. When faced with a tense situation, it's important to remain calm and avoid panic. Straightforward negotiating doesn't always work here and meeting the needs of our residents while maintaining everyone's safety remains a formidable challenge. As a supervisor, I strive to do my best and when things don't go well, I take it personally.

One of my greatest fears is that one day I'll begin to lose my patience with residents through burnout or become so complacent that I just end up going through the motions merely to collect a paycheck. In my field, this is commonly referred to as an "appliance nurse." It's a term that has been around for years and is awarded to those nurses who continue to work only to purchase their "next kitchen appliance". Like many managers/owners, their care factor for others is zero! They're around today more than ever and can be hard to get rid of. Fortunately, I still love my job enough and know when it's time to bow out gracefully. Much of this writing is helping me to express what I experience. As an aspiring author, I thank you for taking the time to read this writing; you are my listening ear.

Following the incident, I briefly meet with my staff to discuss what we could have done differently as a team and how to avoid a reoccurrence. More importantly, I always thank my coworkers for their team effort during another surprise escalation incident. No way would I have been able to handle it without them. It's amazing how rapidly a situation can go south and without a strong supportive cast, you can quickly become overwhelmed. Also, we discussed the need to focus on proper engagement and took some time for Q&A.

Several staff members expressed how uncomfortable they became when Ed began to act out. The topic of honesty also was brought up and how residents will sometimes approach staff with questions about their parents or other family members who are deceased. I explained how in recent years, much controversy has surrounded the issue of being truthful when engaging someone with Alzheimer's. On one hand, we know it's never right to knowingly lie to someone; and yet if we truthfully inform them of a loved one's death, they may break down emotionally by reliving a tragic past event. I carefully explained that redirecting the conversation from the subject long enough will usually cause them to forget the original question thus averting the whole honesty issue. However, knowing *how* to successfully accomplish this involves more than mere verbal interaction.

Effective communication and redirection involves facial expression, tone of voice and body language. Nonverbal cues must exude love, concern, kindness and compassion. While many here may not be as sharp as they once were, they can sense genuineness.

Furthermore, truly relating to them involves understanding interaction from their perspective and what struggles they have. I explained that you must place yourself in their shoes to sincerely appreciate what *they* may be feeling.

With its progression, the disease often renders its victim without the ability to speak correctly, resulting in increased stress—for everyone. This can occur frequently with certain residents, demanding early recognition and intervention by caregivers. Interventions include helping residents spell out words with the use of large print letters. Certain individuals quickly grow frustrated with their inability to clearly articulate their words and thus become angry with their apparent loss of speech. Others may simply chuckle while continuing to stumble over their words. Understanding the need to focus on the cause(s) of anger, rather than the anger itself is important. The ability to accomplish this is what a good memory care unit clinician can do. I must remember that my residents are victims and my job is to help them regardless of how effective my efforts may be.

For training purposes, I'll occasionally conduct a roll play exercise to better equip workers when confronted with difficult situations. I often think back of my days in my high school theater class and hope they're finally beginning to pay off. Also, a resident acting out is often the result of a trigger within their surroundings such as Lucille and her encounter with the mirror. We couldn't identify exactly what caused Ed to insist on meeting his wife. He may have seen someone either on the unit or even on T.V. who reminded him of his late wife. Connecting the dots isn't always so easy; which is why we focus so much on prevention.

Loving the person while despising the behavior is tough. "It's not them," I often tell my coworkers. "It's someone else in their place. This horrible disease has come in and taken this person captive and they have no control of their behavior."

After we broke, Coleen commented, "It's like you've got to hate the disease...but love the person."

Exiting the office, I commended her for her insight and saw in her, a future supervisor.

"You know you're going have my job one day."

"You mean when you come back as a resident?!" I love her sarcasm.

"Exactly!" We laughed.

That afternoon, it dawned on me that I'm the one being educated. Both my staff and residents have taught me the importance of caring for and embracing others when it seems impossible. The difficulties I face force me to flee my comfort zone, make critical thinking decisions and share with staff members my resolution. Feedback allows me to see things from different perspectives thus making me a better supervisor. The best way to understand the inner workings of a memory unit is through exposure to it, but to master it, you must also teach it.

Embracing those who live and work here has left its mark on my heart and has made me a better, more caring person. Sometimes life's most important lessons come to us through our experiences. Handling today's confrontation with Ed put my skills to the test. It proved my competency and educated others on how to handle situations of crisis intervention. This was certainly the silver lining around todays cloud. Understanding the need for growth in this area is crucial and as a team, we can now apply what we've learned and hopefully prevent future occurrences from happening.

Bull Riding

Slowly we begin to feel some normalcy return to the unit while I sign paperwork for over a thousand medication tablets, several cases of undergarments and dozens of body creams. Robin learns firsthand the task of inventory. I explain that we have several pharmacies making deliveries during all hours of the day and how a never-ending process of pill counting, reordering of medications and medical supplies acts to occupy a huge chunk of time.

Next, I familiarize him with the office and how he may wish to prioritize his duties. The phone rings, and I answer using speaker.

"Rembrandt nurses station, how may I help you?"

"Hi, it's Marge, just wanted to let you know today's admission called and said they should be here by six or so. I'll ring again when they arrive. Also, Lori Ann called. She won't be able to come to work tonight…something about a family emergency. I have a call out for a replacement, but haven't heard back yet."

"Okay, we'll find a way to manage. Thanks for the

update."

"You're welcome, bye bye."

"Bye."

"With that call off, I'll need to be on a wagon over in the Van Gogh which means you'll need to pass meds later here in the Rembrandt. Are you okay with that?" I ask.

Robin shot me a look like I was asking him to ride a wild bull. Before he can answer, the door alarm sounds.

"For Pete's sake." I whine, rolling my eyes. "Every day at the exact time, they do the same thing...honestly, I could set my watch by it."

"Who is it?"

"Guess...our trio of troublemakers;

Molly, Thelma and—."

"Let me guess...the Troll?" he interjects.

"Of course!"

Little did he realize he was already on that bull. Exiting the office, a verbal altercation ensues among our three amigos and we quickly separate them while resetting the alarm pad. I hear my office phone ringing and I allow it to go to message while helping Robin and Coleen redirect our would-be fugitives. We coax them back to the executive lounge while they stare at Robin.

"Hey folks, let's all extend a warm welcome to

Robin, our new nurse!" I announce loudly while clapping, as if introducing him on the Tonight Show. A few residents slowly give a clap but most maintain their signature flat affect except for the Troll who can always be counted on to speak her mind.

"You a boy or a girl?" She bellows without batting an eye. Speechless, Coleen and I await a reply while trying not to laugh.

"Hermaphrodite." He grinned, reaching down to stroke Mr. Robinson.

"I didn't ask what religion you were; I asked if you're a boy or girl!" she shouted angrily.

"Sally, you need to settle down if ..." I interjected.

Performing her signature turn, she quickly waddled away. Trying my best to keep a straight face I thought, he's just experienced his first confrontation with the Troll. Carefully, we help Jo Ann, Lucille and the others to sit and watch Bowling for Dollars.

"Is this what they usually watch?" he asked.

"At this time, yea. But later, we have karaoke or maybe we'll show an old movie. We have a million DVD's and CD's to choose from, they're in the activities office next to the dining hall so feel free to pop in whatever you want. Also, we hand out snacks around eight before they go to bed."

"What kind of snacks?"

"Oh, well on movie nights we hand out nachos or popcorn, and the ones without choppers enjoy yogurt, pudding, or applesauce."

"Baked goods...like brownies?

"Sure...or cookies...for special occasions we usually have ice cream and cake. Most all of them love sweets.

"Yes, at Westly Home, my previous employer, we made brownies at least twice a week or so...helps to keep the weight on them.

"That's a great idea because some like, Lucille and Emma, cannot seem to gain even an ounce. But watch Sally. She'll cannibalize the whole batch if she's able."

"Yea, I kind of got that impression." He smirked.

Before leaving, I took time to introduce him to a few others on the couch, including Crack Shot, Saucy Smile, Little Minx and the Colonel. He fully knew his nursing skills were about to be put to the test and I felt for him as I knew he wasn't told the truth in his interview about what to expect once he hit the floor. Pushing the wagon back to the office I provide some pointers on where to begin his med pass along with how to administer to certain residents. Also, I explain how lots of close interaction is often necessary along with the use of the flags and sedatives and if things get too heated, to call for me.

Once in my office, I notice the light on my phone flashing and suddenly remember about Marge calling when our admission arrived. What I playback are several anxious messages left by both Carol and Marie indicating that state inspectors have arrived and are currently at the entrance. Knowing they could be here at any moment, I speed dial Carol and leave her a voice mail that I'll be on the lookout and any expired meds will be discarded ASAP. After erasing her message, we head to the rear of my office.

"Those meds we're supposed to get rid of are back there." I say, pointing to the storage closet. Robin nods while surveying the crowded mess just inside the entry door. Quickly, we clear a pathway through the cluttered mess. We're having to navigate around old fax machines, computer monitors, office furniture and file cabinets. Located at the rear, we discover two large louvered folding doors along with a strong musty odor.

"When I worked overnights we always emptied the bottles and bubble packs into trash bags for disposal, but I don't see them...wish we had more light...I don't know why overnights haven't taken care of this...this is ridiculous!" My iPhone flashlight feature helps, but

Robin has what we need, a laser pen.

"What's in there?" He asks pointing his red laser toward the rear.

"You got me...the meds, I hope."

Footing is soon made difficult as loose pills litter the carpeted floor with a notable concentration towards the rear. After repositioning the last of several file cabinets, we finally have access to the louvered panels. In near dark conditions, we discover two quarter-sized porcelain knobs, each located at eye level and tightly wired together. Efforts to loosen the thin metal cable are futile due to our inability to gain a grip but fortunately we're able to at least jiggle loose one of the knobs.

Without warning, both doors violently fly open releasing a tsunami of loose medications. Within seconds, we're on our keesters, buried up to necks in pills, tablets, capsules, suppositories and Lord knows what else. Speechless, we stared at each other in disbelief.

"Aaaaah...I don't believe it...you okay?...we gotta bag these up!" I yelled. "Quick, follow me...come on!" Frantically we dig our way out, dragging a sea of medications with us. "Don't get any in the hallway...hurry!"

Once outside the office, I'm unable to fully close my door. "What the heck!" Pulling with all my strength I'm growing impatient when two tall gentlemen dressed like homicide investigators suddenly confront us.

"Excuse me, do either of you know where we can find the charge nurse?"

"Ah...yes sir, that would be me." I answer hearing the door *click* shut.

"Good afternoon, we're from the Agency for Health Care Administration...can we please see...your certificate of licensure and any resident charts you maintain...is this your office ...can we go inside please?"

Robin and I just looked at each other realizing our fate. Unable to open what only moments before seemed impossible to close, I again begin struggling with the door when suddenly the fire alarm sounds—saved by the bell! Immediately, I radio the aides to ensure all residents remain in their rooms and that all fire doors to be fully closed.

After hearing Laura and Coleen return my call, I turn to the inspectors. "Gentlemen, I'm sorry but per company policy, all non-resident personnel are required to exit the building whenever the threat of a fire exist. Please follow us."

Speechless, they look at each other exactly as Robin and I did only moments before. Anxiously, we escorted them down the closest stairwell exit before returning to my office. Enroute, we briefly stopped to grab some trash bags from the closet across the hall.

"Hey, is that a shop vac?...grab it, it's just what we need!"

"Got it".

Once back, we discover the door jamming problem was due to medications that had lodged in the door frame.

"Looks like you found a new way to crush meds...got ne' applesauce?" Robin commented; we both busted out laughing. We knew we just dodged a career-ending incident and now seemed to thumb our nose at it. Like kids, we snickered about the situation, and for the first time I feel comfortable with him. No longer did I see him as just *another* new hire, but rather as a friend. I'd learned firsthand the lesson to never judge a book by its cover. Once inside, we discover the Troll rummaging through the loose medications and Mr. Robinson chewing what appears to be an Exlax tablet.

"How they'd get in here?" He asks.

"Who knows?"

Escorting her out is met with great resistance as Mr. Robinson looked on, wide eyed and curious about the mountain of medications. Next, I call Marge and she confirms the fire alarm is only a drill. Bagging up the meds, the alarm stops and we scramble knowing the inspectors could return at any moment. Despite the shop vacs' capacity of twenty gallons, we filled it to the brim along with several bags before stashing everything back in the utility closet.

Awaiting the inspectors return, we quickly review the report log and the admission paperwork. Nearly ten minutes pass and still neither inspector show—only the Troll—curious about Robin, and looking for more meds.

"I have to meet with Tina to see what we missed in the meeting. If I'm more than ten or fifteen minutes, I'll call you on my radio. If those inspectors show, call me on the phone at either the central nurses station or the clinic. Thanks again for all your help, you did an awesome job with everything."

"Sure thing."

Heading out I think; he can ride a bull quite well.

Clothing Optional

Once on the AL side, I make a beeline for the nurse's station. Entering, I notice Tina on the phone gathering a large stack of papers. After hanging up, she asks in a loud whisper;

"What happened?

"Ed, determined on going to meet his wife…again!"

"Oh, I've dealt with that before. He can be scary."

"Yeah, you're not kidding."

I explained the fiasco, but never got to the Viagra Volcano due to "Jack Friday" and his accomplice, who were now hovering just outside the clinic—talking to Jane.

"I forgot all about having that stupid drill to-day…and I was there when maintenance scheduled it! And now these inspectors …what the heck's going on?"

Before I can respond, she again quickly interjects, "Oh, you're not gonna *believe* what happened up here!" Her signature raising eyebrow gets my attention.

"What?"

"Jane was let go."

"What!"

"I know, it came as a shock to me as well." She responded.

"Apparently after our meeting broke, Carol and Marie asked her to hang for a moment, and when she came out, she was crying. Sherri said they'd made the decision last week to terminate her, but I think she knew she had it coming...she was written up three times last month...what do you expect?"

"Yeah...well, that's par for the course around here." I add. "But who's going to replace her?" Suddenly it hit me, knowing her termination was coming and given her taste for revenge, she must have called the state.

"Robin, I guess."

"Robin...Robin doesn't *know* our residents." I snapped.

"Exactly, but they don't have a choice...they do this all the time...looks like he'll be shadowing you tonight." Her familiar smirk takes over.

Knowing she's eager to leave, I grab the report log. "Speaking of Robin." I whisper.

"He's actually pretty cool. I'll explain later." She provides me a quick verbal report along with a list of residents who've yet to return from appointments.

"I finished all but this last lab order and...the rest

you can read...I've got to go; my son has a dental appointment and Carol is really on us about the overtime."

"I know...I heard it last week from Marie about punching out time."

"Thanks." she says with an exhaustive sigh.

"Busy day...huh?" I ask.

"Crazy." She says exhaling. What she needs most is a glass of merlot and a massage.

"Hasta mañana" She exits.

Some days it's a great feeling to leave here and for Tina, today is one of those days.

Scanning the lab order to be faxed, I notice Delores' name at the top of the page. Awaiting the transmittal receipt, I finish reading the report log and check for phone messages. Preparing for my med pass, I begin stocking my wagon, when a call comes on my radio.

"Assistance needed in Rembrandt...
Day area...please!"

I recognized the voice as Robin's.

"On my way." I respond.

Entering the unit, all is quiet. Heading to the executive lounge, I'm met with the aroma of incense; a smell which transports me back to my teenage years. Not an odor I'm used to back here, I think as I hear the door lock behind me.

Arriving at the lounge I observe residents enjoying tonight's karaoke hour. Only a glance towards the far seating area revealed Robin's need for assistance. During the completion of "Puff the Magic Dragon", Josephine elected to remove both her blouse and brassiere. This can appear shocking to some and understandably so. I watch as Laura and Robin worked gently yet persistently with her to get her clothes back on.

Could one imagine being in public and watch with disbelief as someone disrobed? This of course can be expected in a setting such as our memory unit and isn't that big of a deal for those who work here. However, for visitors, the experience can be shocking. Interestingly, despite someone baring it all in the center of a crowded room, the reaction of those seated around her was one of complete indifference except for the Troll, who simply stared quietly without expression. I would have given a million bucks to know what she was thinking. I return to the kitchen area and pour myself a fresh cup of Joe when Robin enters.

"Well *that* was interesting." I say in a comical tone.

"Yeah." He responds. "I just finished seating residents when I looked up to see her bare breasted."

"Those inspectors ever come back?" I ask.

"No, not yet."

I can tell he's still processing the strip tease.

"We'd better keep a close eye on her." I add. "She's only been here about three months but has really staged these last couple of weeks. She gave us a scare the other day when she became non-responsive, and today, she wouldn't take her meds for Tina."

"Could be a UTI, or just staging," He responded "I'll get a urine sample on her tonight and call the lab."

"Yeah if you can, that would be great. By the way, is that...incense I smell?"

"Yes, essences of incense to be exact; I call it solutions for sun downing. It's a plug-in aromatherapy. We used it at Westly Home—a lot. It can be really effective."

"Awesome." I reply, wondering what else he has in store.

"I think it helps calm them down. Boy, that one you call The Troll...she's something else."

"Oh yeah!" I reply. "She can really grind your gears."

"How long has she been here?"

"About...five years now. When she arrived, we had to hire agency for nearly a month—just to follow her. She would constantly get into trouble. Her favorite thing used to be clogging toilets with rolls of toilet tissue. Last week she snuck out behind a linen cart and was discovered in laundry services instructing the staff on how to iron cloths. They thought she was a supervisor in house-keeping."

"You're kidding."

"No, I'm dead serious, she's unbelievable!"

He gives a slow wag of his head while letting go a belly laugh. "Yeah, we had one like her at Westly Home. You just gotta know how best to deal with them."

I wasn't exactly sure about what he meant by "best," but remained interested in what I'd eventually discover.

"How's it out in the Van Gogh?" He asks.

I want to share about Jane being canned, but feel it too gossipy. I look for something to say when suddenly the lights flicker.

"Uh oh!" We quickly look up at the overhead lights, anticipating darkness.

"Hope we don't have a repeat of the other night. Residents were wandering the halls asking when we would have power, it was a mess. We were on the generator till almost midnight. Maintenance said it nearly ran out of gas."

"Really—what do we do if that happens?"

"I don't know, I just hope they filled the tank. I'm sorry, you asked me something; oh yeah, the Van Gogh. Well, so far so good. We got the lab back on our oldest one, Delores. Her bilateral ankle edema is back. It's her congested heart failure. I'm surprised she lasted this long."

"I remember seeing her on the report." He adds. "What's her room number?"

"Seventy-seven."

"And how old is she?"

"One o' eight…in about three weeks.

"wow!

"Yeah, she was in grade school when *The Titanic* went down."

"How's her quality of life?"

"Not bad, she's in the Van Gogh, which is surprising. Usually by that age they're either in Skilled Nursing, or here in the memory unit."

"Exactly." He adds.

"It looks like they'll increase her water pill and potassium." I say searching for more creamer. "I've got to call Marge about our admission before I head back to the Van Gogh. I'll see ya later."

"Hey, here's another creamer," he says tossing it to me.

"Thanks." Secretly, I like the aromatherapy, but know it will never fly with the Marionettes.

Till Death Do We Part

Heading to my office I hear the doorbell. Outside I see a tall, slightly disheveled gentleman accompanied by an attractive well-dressed lady. Thinking this must be our admission; I quickly disarm the door and invite them in.

"Hello, welcome to the Rembrandt, my name is Ken. You must be Steve and Merri." I say, extending my arm. His six-foot plus frame and broad shoulders give him a noticeable presence. Wearing a purple polo and khakis, he is a handsome gentleman with a full head of silver hair, bushy salt-and-pepper eyebrows and mustache. Introducing myself, he creases a smile while slowly extending his hand; he doesn't have time to answer.

"Yes—and I'm Merri." she responds nervously. Her appearance is perfect. She's extremely pulled together and then it hits me, I'm looking at Florence Henderson's twin. I invite them into my office.

"Would either of you like something to drink? We have coffee, tea or bottled water?"

"Oh, no thanks. We're okay. Unless do you want anything, dear?" Steve tries to process, but again isn't given time.

"No, we're fine. But thank you anyway."

"Have a seat, please. I'm glad to see you made it here safe and sound. I know the weather these past few days has been crazy. Was it raining when you came in?"

"Just starting to." She responds.

"Okay, well again, welcome to the Rembrandt. I'd like to discuss a few things and then we'll take a tour of our unit. Also, I'll need to get Steve's vital signs and the date of his last doctor's visit.

"Yes, his last appointment with his primary was yesterday and…I'll have to check when he last saw the neurologist." She answers nervously, tapping her iPhone.

His illness rests squarely on her shoulders. Her Stepford look helps to disguise her anguish, but Steve's vacant stare gives it away. She's powerless against the disease but like so many before her, will not give in without a fight. She's become his eyes, ears, and voice and is doing her best to survive.

"Oh, that's okay, his primary is just fine." I respond. "I reviewed Steve's info earlier and see where he was found walking in your neighborhood…unsure of how to get back home."

"Yes, it was last Friday. He always feeds the squirrels after breakfast; don't you Hun," She gives a nod, attempting to visually cue him.

We look at Steve for several moments.

"Squirrels, yes, I like, I like to." He stutters.

I continue to try and connect visually with Steve, but to no avail. He wages a silent battle against an enemy that is slowly consuming him and to which there remains no proven cure.

"I called for him." She says. "But, he didn't answer. I looked everywhere. Finally, I got in the car and found him…on the next street over…"

Overwhelmed with emotion, she can't speak. I place my hand on hers and reach for a Kleenex.

"I just figured he was still out front. I never imagined he would wander off."

Handing her a tissue, I glance at Steve. He knows Merri is upset, but isn't sure why.

The phone rings and I allow it to go to message while pushing the do not disturb feature. Before I can speak, my radio blares. "Rembrandt nurses station, call the front desk!"

"Please excuse me one moment."

I phone Marge who reminds me of tonight's water shutoff scheduled for eight pm. Hanging up, a loud knock comes at the door. It's Robin.

"Sorry to interrupt, but can I get the med cart keys—please?"

"Sure. I apologize; I forgot to give them to you earlier."

"No worries." He replies.

"Merri, Steve this is Robin…he's one of our nurses." Handing him the keys, Merri smiles and does a double take at Robin as Steve shakes his hand.

"Thanks." He exits.

An awkward silence dominates the room. With so many interruptions, I decide to pick up on Steve's elopement story later.

"Tell you what, let's tour the unit and get Steve situated, and when we are all done, we can talk more."

"That would be great." She responds.

Despite the interruptions, I feel our meeting went well and I know Merri is eager to talk. Our brief silence is broken by the Troll shouting at Robin about her medications along with the exit-door alarm sounding.

Slowly we stand and prepare to head for Steve's apartment. This part is always awkward as Steve will be introduced to what likely will be—his final residence.

Leaving my office, Coleen approaches with vanilla ice-cream smothered in warm chocolate syrup; a little perk we do for newcomers and their family. It works to help break the ice and is exactly what Steve and Merri needed.

Making our way toward the lounge area, we encounter Mr. Robinson along with residents who notice these new faces and pause to stare. Sensing Merri's uneasiness, I take time to introduce them.

"Good evening, ladies, this is Steve…and Merri…"

Lucille and the others only gaze at them while admiring the change in scenery. Steve fixated on Mr. Robinson, gently snapped his fingers and bent over to befriend our mascot. Merri retained her tense smile while coddling her frozen treat before giving a sheepish h-e-l-l-o. Continuing, we take a brief tour of the unit while I explain its layout along with scheduled times for meals, activities, and medications. I see the Troll approaching and make a quick detour for Steve's apartment.

In his room, I ask Coleen to head her off at the door, and she does so just in time.

"So how are you feeling today Steve?" With no answer, I look at him, pause and repeat the question. "So how are you doing …today?

"Well, I guess I'm being put out to pasture," he replies while looking down.

I was shocked! It was the first time I clearly heard his voice; it was that of a country western singer who needed to clear his throat. His answer says it all; I thought, not only for him but for millions of seniors across our nation. An early lesson on what lies ahead—for many of us.

Newcomers will sometimes feel abandoned in addition to moving one step closer to the grave. Initially, some battle depression and isolation, which compound other problems associated with AD, such as sun downing or accelerated cognitive decline. Steve's response certainly communicated his feelings about being relocated here. Helping him adjust to this paradigm shift is an ongoing process that may take weeks and even months to achieve. In rare cases, some individuals are never able to adjust and remain bitter and resentful.

Becoming familiar with his new surroundings in addition to being embraced by a loving staff will help to soften his adjustment. Also, decompensation of his memory and overall brain cognition will result in the eventual acceptance of his new home.

During my time with Steve, I will need to complete a head-to-toe assessment. This evaluation will involve obtaining vital signs, checking his skin for cuts or sores, reviewing current medications and asking questions which in turn will give me a better idea of how advanced his dementia is. I begin with his career.

"So how long have you been retired?"

"Oh...about..." struggling to answer, he turns to Merri.

"Five and a half years...from American Airlines...he was a pilot." She replies with a nervous smile.

"Really...my dad was a pilot for Eastern." I shot back. "Do you miss it?"

I notice Merri with a worried look, wanting to answer, but knowing she should allow Steve. Speaking of my dad filled the silence.

"He always said there are three rules to a good landing...unfortunately though, no one knows what they are."

"Except for Sully." Steve commented, scraping his last spoon of ice cream.

Merri giggled and commented "That's true."

"I just don't understand why I'm here," he blurted.

"So, we can help you, Steve." I respond encouragingly. "As you grow older, you're going to need help with some things, and that's what we do...we can do all the work for you while you sit back and relax—okay?" I say, applying a blood pressure cuff on his upper arm.

"How...how much is this all going to cost?" he stuttered with a look of suspicion.

"That was all taken care of when you came in." I say inflating the blood pressure cuff. "I'm the one in charge and if you need anything, you ask for me."

He gave a gentle nod and seemed to deflate along with the BP cuff, now hanging loosely on his arm. Moments later, he repeated the question, and I repeated my response.

"Where's my Merri?" He called.

Quickly, Merri stepped over and took hold of his hand. "I'm right here hun."

"Oh...there you...are." Slowly his fearful look waned as Merri moved to embrace him.

After helping him disrobe, I conclude a skin check and listen to his lungs and heart before taking his temperature. Seeing he has a wristwatch, I ask him for the time and date. This is done to determine a baseline of his current cognitive abilities and will be addressed again in the coming months to verify how quickly he may be staging. I start with the time.

"Steve, can you tell me what time you have, please?"

"Six...six..." He looks at Merri.

"It's six twenty-one." Merri quickly answered as a

soft tap came at the door.

I realized that at least a portion of my assessment will be best accomplished after Merri departs. At the door is Coleen who returns with bed linens and offers to assist Steve with unpacking. Silence dominates the room, and I sense Merri growing nervous. Suddenly Mr. Robinson jumped into Steve's lap. We hadn't even noticed that he entered the room and were all taken by surprise. His timing couldn't have been better to distract Steve as Merri was now confronted with saying goodbye. She's aware that if she informs him of her leaving, he'll begin to question why he isn't going with her.

Gathering up my B/P cuff, stethoscope and clipboard, I ask Steve to assist Coleen with unpacking after he's done getting acquainted with Mr. Robinson. Cordially he agrees and as Coleen takes over, Merri and I sneak out.

Back at my office, she shared with me about being in denial and how she's struggled lately to accept his limitations. She didn't speak any more about his elopement, and I didn't ask. I give her what she needs; a listening ear.

"He just can't remember a thing. His mind, it's like a sieve, really, I mean he can't even set the table or...anything. The other night he emptied the dish washer and filled the cabinets with dirty dishes and the silverware drawer with dirty silverware. And now he's...wandering off! He doesn't even understand why I'm so upset half the time; it's like living with a *two*-year-old. I love him to death but, it's so much work. I didn't want to bring him here but...I just can't do this any longer, he's driving me crazy!"

Overwhelmed with emotion, she pauses. Her acceptance of his placement here may become easier over time but a certain emptiness will always remain. Helping her deal with such a life changing event is probably the most challenging and yet rewarding part of my job. She's having to process so much so quickly while learning the painful lesson of letting go. There is so much I want to say but I don't dare speak. Her cell phone rings. She looks to see the caller and politely whispers;

"I'm sorry, I have to get this."

I respond with thumbs up and start writing my admission note on Steve. After several minutes, she hangs up.

"I'm so sorry but our granddaughter's in the hospital, and I have to go. I'll be back later."

With so much unsaid, we quickly hug and I see her to the door. Exiting, she gives a quick wave and heads for the elevator.

My heart aches for her as she is torn apart emotionally and is wrestling with guilt and remorse. Today allowed little time for me to comfort Merri in the way she needs—by listening. I feel her pain. After finishing my intake entry on Steve, I quickly jot myself a note to call her by nine o'clock in case I don't hear from her. Resetting the do not disturb feature on my phone, I receive a call.

"Good Evening, Rembrandt nurses station."

"Hi, this is Candi at Saint Agnes Hospital. I'm trying to reach the nurse for Calvin Richards."

"Yes! That's me...how is he?

"Well, stable, but he's being transferred to CCC." (Critical Cardiac Care) "Can you fax over his H and P (History and Physical) and any next of kin?"

"Sure, what's you fax number?" Grabbing his chart, a large lump forms in my throat. Before she can answer, a loud crack of thunder is herd, the lights flicker and the line goes dead.

"Well that's just great!" I snap. Quickly, I check the call log and speed dial her back. The number goes to a recording which instructs me to leave a message but also provides a fax number. I fax Calvin's H and P while checking his family contacts. I soon realize that he has none listed. The only number in his chart was the one I called earlier following his transport out—his POA. Next, I fax his demographics and redial Candi but still get the recording. This time I leave a message asking her to confirm if she received my faxes. Patiently I wait, but no call.

Easily Ms. Handled

Captain Kangaroo indicates it's now seven pm and I'm needing to dispense meds in the Van Gogh. Prior to leaving, I peek in and see Steve talking with Laura, enjoying his second helping of ice cream, and stroking Mr. Robinson, who has taken extremely well to our newcomer.

Laura patiently assists him with his breakfast menu repeating each item several times before deciding on what he likes best. His new home will take some getting used to, but with time, he'll adjust nicely. He's a gentle soul who's aging gracefully and I'm looking forward to talking with him about his flying career.

Heading for the Van Gogh, I see Robin's acquired an entourage of residents including the Troll who's assisting with pushing the wagon. Also, he's introduced mood lighting by dimming the overheads in the lounge area and has selected John Lennon's "Imagine" as background music. Not a bad idea...I think as things do appear calmer. Exiting, I hear laughter erupt from his wagon and laugh a little myself. Hmmm, something else

I'm not used to back here...laughter.

Back in the Van Gogh, I receive an urgent page from Marge about a physician who's been placed on hold. It's about Delores's low potassium lab results and the need to order medications. Following the call, I fax the STAT order to the local pharmacy while completing the paperwork along with additional orders.

Again, the lights flicker and suddenly I'm in the dark. With my iPhone light feature, I open the first-aid closet and locate a flashlight, which provides the illumination of a birthday candle. Soon we have power back and I quickly swap out the batteries before broadcasting to my coworkers of the need to locate a flashlight and keep it handy.

Running so far behind, I quickly review the twenty-four- hour log and locate my med-cart keys. Next, I head for the end of a long hall where I notice a resident peering from her apartment like a meerkat on the Serengeti, checking if it's safe to come out. Passing the dining room, I faintly hear a concerto by Mozart along with the clanging of silverware and china as residents enjoy their favorite dessert.

Tonight's reassignment to the Van Gogh entails more than simply giving residents their pills. It's about continuity of care and critical thinking as I'm the eyes and ears of every resident's physician. Simple interaction allows me to identify areas of possible concern. These areas include: changes in general appearance such as skin color and odor; changes in cognition like memory or recall; and changes in motor skills such as increased difficulty with balance or changes in gait. Additionally, I may be privileged with hearing a good joke.

I haven't worked this location of the AL for nearly three weeks and can't say I've missed it. I've no doubt grown accustomed to the insane pace required in the Rembrandt, and now time has suddenly slowed to a crawl. It's like leaving a busy ER to work at Hospice House.

Located at the end is apartment fifty-one, home of Virginia, our meerkat who, as per the report log, occupies her doorway every evening waiting to interrogate whoever rolls up. Her relocation here comes after losing her husband to a rare, inoperable brain cancer. She prefers to eat in her room and rarely participants in activities. Last week in collaborative care we discussed how she's bored out of her mind yet refuses to get out and make friends. My arrival is likely the highlight of her day and instead of watching *Family Feud* or *Wheel of Fortune*, it looks like I'll be tonight's entertainment.

Like many newcomers, she'll probably talk my ear

off and may even follow me as I hand out pills—the part of my job that can either be intriguing—or incredibly tiresome. Approaching, I notice her bright red floral bathrobe and pink fuzzy slippers. Coming to a stop I *feel* her stare. She sports a shaggy bob with thinning gray bangs, beady eyes, and an adorable button nose. A strong gust of wind might just knock her over.

"Hello, how are you today…?"

Her stare intensifies.

"You must be Virginia." Again, I pause.

"Ginny…I go by Ginny." Her voice creaks like an antique hinge. "I don't remember seeing you before."

"I'm not usually on this floor." I respond. "I mostly work the memory unit…although I don't remember why." My comedic response sails over her head.

"Well…it's good to meet you." Her look softens. "So you're gonna give me my pill tonight?"

"Yes ma'am, give me just a moment and I'll see what you get." I quickly review her schedule. "It's only the one…and it's a sleeper, what time do you go to bed?"

"Not till later, but you can just leave it with me now. That will save you a trip…Lori always gives it to me early."

Being so far behind, I decide to bend the rules a bit

and give her the pill when suddenly I discover her supply to be out.

"I'm sorry, Ginny, but I have to get a new bottle from the clinic...I guess they forgot to stock the cart this morning."

"You mean you can't give me my pill...I have to have my pill to sleep!" She fired back.

"Yes, yes I just have to get more from the clinic, but don't worry, you'll get your pill by eight o'clock."

"Okay, as long as it's by eight."

I'm curious about Ginny. She appears alert but I'm not sure if she's all with it. I need to take a closer look at her but I'm also needing to dispense dozens of medications in addition to completing my rounds. Seeing she's in no real distress, I decide to continue administering meds and assess her when I return with her pill.

"Yes ma'am, I'll see you then." I can tell she's not ready for me to leave.

As I begin pushing my cart, she mentions something about her late husband when my radio suddenly drowns her out.

"Nurse needed in room twenty-five...fall!" I recognized the caller as Monique and before I can answer,

Robin responds.

"On my way."

Pandemonium is heard in the background and I begin to feel guilty about leaving Robin, but with tonight's call off, I've no choice. I promptly acknowledge the call and instruct him to radio me if he needs help and he acknowledges. Soon, other residents begin to congregate around my wagon.

"Hey, when do we get our pills?" Demands one in a crotchety tone.

"Yeah, I've already eaten and I usually take mine before dinner, where's what's her name...Lori Ann, she usually has my pills ready by now!" Barks another.

Suddenly a third resident, Edsel, briskly approaches in his turbocharged scooter, nearly hitting the others. He's another feisty senior enjoying his third childhood with plenty of attitude and no impulse control. Coming to an abrupt stop, he announces; "My butt holes on fire...ever have that problem?"

"No."

"Well, give me sompin' for it. I can't stand it!"

Angrily, the others protest. "Hey, wait a minute, Joyce and I were here first, his butt hole can wait...where's our pills?"

Some here will step over a dead body to get their

pills. As they continued bickering, I promptly dispensed their meds while trying to follow Ginny. She continues eulogizing her late husband, ignoring the others.

"...and yesterday would have been our anniversary...seventy years . . ."

I hand the last medication to Edsel, an unopened red and yellow tube of cream. I tell him I'll be in later to assess his bottom and he speeds away.

"Seventy years...wow...that's a long time." I continue, pouring pills and documenting while trying to absorb all she has to say.

"...Nineteen forty-four." She continues. "He's gone now... cancer took him." I feel an awkward silence.

"I'm so sorry...I can tell you really miss him...where did you two meet?" Anxious to get going, I try to lighten the discussion by finishing on a good note.

"In high school, during the war. He volunteered to go...he was in the Normandy Invasion and Battle of the Bulge...he was a purple heart." Her only smile reveals a loose-fitting partial plate.

"You must be so proud." Before rolling away, I offer a gentle hug and she accepts. Stepping toward her, I notice a slight tremor of her hand along with her complexion, which appears pasty. Her gaunt look, puffy lips, and halitosis all seemed to hit me at once and embracing her

I notice she feels, skeletal? My med pass is officially now on hold! I look to see Monique approaching from down the hall and Ginny quickly retreats into her doorway. Reaching for the BP cuff on the wagon, Monique arrives and noticing my look, realizes something's up.

"I just came to tell you about Edsel." She rolls her eyes. "He's having a conniption about his bottom and wants to see you now!"

"I know, he just left here, I'll be down when I can...who fell?"

"Oh, that was Victoria, a-g-a-i-n! Robin got her up; you know how she fakes her falls by layin' down and then plays possum...yea...he'll talk to you when you come down to see Edsel. But she's fine."

"How's Robin making out down there?"

"He's having a great time! He got the karaoke machine out and managed to get them all clapping. He asked me if we have a mixing bowl...I said to try the pantry next to activities."

She gives Ginny the once over. "Honey, your color doesn't look so good...how are you feeling?" Monique asks placing her hand on Ginny's forehead.

"Oh, I'm okay...really I'm just fine...can you get me

my pill…dear?"

Monique and I look at each other and I can tell she's just as curious about Ginny. Knowing she's not, *just fine,* it's now up to me to discover the truth, and Monique's timing couldn't have been better. Tag teaming with another worker is usually effective when trying to get a resident to fess up. Gently Monique takes hold of her hand, checking her pulse while I slowly velcro a B/P cuff to her upper arm.

"Ginny, hun, we need to check you out. You look haggard."

"Why?" Her look of suspicion returns.

"Well, we're concerned about you, dear…have you eaten today…you feel warm."

"I'm always cold…sure wish you'd all turn up the heat around here."

With some resistance, she allows us to obtain her vitals, but vehemently denies me the chance to listen to her lungs.

"My lungs are fine, and I'm not getting undressed so you can do whatever…just give me my pill so I can go to sleep!"

By now it's obvious she's hiding something, probably major, and I'm needing to find out what. Interestingly, Ginny does not want to be assessed—and if I can't assess—I can't treat. I must do what's right for Ginny, but I also must have her permission. This means navigating the waters of role reversal; a term used to describe a contemporary who has the audacity to tell an elder what she should do. Smooth sailing is a rarity.

If I can only keep her warm, I can further my assessment...I think but how? Suddenly, I remember a trick my mom used on her mother. When Grandma complained of stripping down before her shower, mom found a solution; create a makeshift sauna!

I decide no longer is it time to say what needs to be done, but rather just act. Slowly, Monique and I gently coaxed Ginny into her bathroom while explaining how she would remain warm while we listened to her lungs. Once in, we're met with a pungent odor and we began running the hot water. Soon we have a steam room and she can disrobe comfortably.

"I'm not takin' a shower!" She shouted, slowly removing her robe.

"You don't have to, dear. We just want to listen to your lungs," Monique and I reiterated.

I feel shocked and nauseated at the site of Ginny. Her body was that of a young child with every bone grossly protruding. Although I don't know Ginny's baseline for being so underweight, she appears to be in a state of starvation. Next comes a loud knock at the door; additional residents wanting their meds. Before Monique can even turn to get a close look at Ginny, she exits to address the knock.

"I'll get them their meds." She announces as I hand her my med cart keys.

"Ginny...why...why do you look like this?" I ask. She hesitates.

"Like what...there's nothing wrong with me...I've always looked like this...and I'm not taking a shower!"

Arguing is of no use. Her denial has her hostage and any demands will only cause her to escalate. Monique returns and making her way through the steam, notices Ginny.

"Ginny!" Her jaw dropping; "What happened to you?"

Slowly I reach to shut off the shower. Ginny looked down without a word, as if being scolded by her granddaughter. Although we wanted answers, now was not the time for interrogation but rather love and support. Monique embraced her while I listened to her breathing. Her lung sounds are clear but with shallow rapid breaths. Her heart rate and rhythm were irregular and I knew it would only be a matter of time before she would develop more serious cardiac arrhythmias, pneumonia and Lord knows what else.

"Ginny, if you don't see a doctor tonight, it could land you in the hospital, for a *very* long time."

Her expression froze. "Well...do you really think it's necessary...I mean..."

"Yes, I do!"

"Can't I just go tomorrow?"

"No!" Monique and I give her the look with laser precision. "If you don't get help, you're going to wither completely away...to say nothing of becoming very sick."

Monique interjects. "Besides, if you don't get looked at, we'll be written up for not doing our job."

"Well...I don't want either of you in trouble...but my pill...I need my pill!"

"When you return...I'll have it right here for you." Finally, with her head hung low she confirmed what we needed, her resignation.

"I'll call for a transport." Monique whispers before exiting.

Giving in to those who are younger can feel like such defeat—a painful lesson experienced by countless elders.

Years of working with our senior population has

taught me that a significant number of them are not candid when confronted with questions about their well-being. Like Ginny, some will cover up, deny, and even lie to keep from exposing a valid health concern. Exactly why is anyone's guess, but over the years I've discovered a recurring theme. Some are deathly afraid of a transport to the hospital for fear they'll never return.

When our residents were young, they learned that many died in hospitals, and now that reality haunts them. Others will risk becoming gravely ill simply to avoid the cost of a doctor's visit.

Raised in the depression era compounds the problem due to the devastating financial strain they may have experienced growing up. With enough apple cider vinegar and honey or Cod liver oil and Epsom salt, they can cure almost anything. If home remedies fail to work, then a kind of ignore it, and maybe "it will go away" syndrome sets in until, like Ginny, they're forced to succumb to the consequences—of their choices.

But for those in the Van Gogh, I believe the greatest fear is ending up in Gods waiting room, a skilled nursing facility (SNF)like the one next door to us. Following a discharge from the hospital, residents must demonstrate enough independence to return here. Should they fail to do so, they're admitted to a SNF, which can mean making the Obits page sooner than expected. Like Ginny, they become masters at trying to avoid the inevitable by skirting around assessments, appointments, and wellness checks. Regardless of the reason, ensuring residents receive optimal care continues to be a challenge for me, and tonight is no exception.

Over the years my skills as a clinician have improved significantly but every now and then I'll be stumped by what I see. Helping residents with hidden concerns begins with gaining their trust, and new admissions are often reluctant to confide in what essentially are strangers.

Feelings of loneliness and isolation can easily lead to health issues like nutritional deficiencies and weight loss. Recognizing and addressing a problem is only the beginning. Identifying the root cause and intervening is where the challenge lies. Certain newcomers can be very private about feeling depressed and tend to clam up when confronted with questions about their emotional well-being. Like Ginny, they may talk your ear off but shy away from discussing valid health concerns. With the recent loss of her husband, she's is no doubt working through the stages of grief and is likely experiencing a low point while adjusting to her relocation here. What lies beyond is anyone's guess.

Understanding why a resident exhibits certain behaviors is sometimes hard to determine. Occasionally some are embarrassed over things such as feminine issues or feeling constipated and refrain from communicating their needs. Others however, work overtime by describing in great detail both the look and feel of their hemorrhoids. In either case, we must establish a firm level of trust or certain residents will no doubt go untreated. Tonight, Ginny handed me my critical thinking cap and Monique helped me put it on.

Ginny is transported to Saint Agnus where she is admitted for severe dehydration, malnutrition, and weakness. Next I'm having to secure her apartment by ensuring her entry door is locked and all lights are out. Again, I'm met with the mysterious nasty smell. Entering her bedroom, I notice everything to be out of sorts. Scattered about the floor are articles of clothing, magazines, empty candy boxes, newspapers and a medication tablet next to her bedside night stand. The pill is the sleep aid—the one she obsessed over prior to leaving.

Entering her bathroom to flush the tablet, I discover the source of the stench; stale vomit lining the inside rim of her toilet. Why the heck hasn't housekeeping cleaned this apartment...I think flushing the tablet. Here she's been sick...and never said anything to us—or so I thought.

I'd later learned she'd been refusing housekeeping services since moving in. Reaching to turn off a table lamp, I stoop to retrieve a pen and several loose pieces of notebook paper. What I discover next caused a noticeable chill to run down my spine.

It's time now for me to go and be with my Bob who's waiting for me. He loves me and we were meant to be together forever. I miss him terribly and don't want to be alone anymore. I'm not going to stay here and nobody can make me so don't try.

Welling up, reading became difficult as a noticeable lump began to form in my throat. Scribbled diagonally on the upper left corner of the page was what looked to be *Wilsons Funeral Home* along with an illegible phone number.

Before finishing, I began to wonder, how exactly did she intend on killing herself? Does she have a gun in here? Then I remembered the pill I'd found. Searching her bedside table drawer, I discovered a denture cup to be nearly full of the same medication which she stashed, probably after telling Lori Ann that she'd take them later.

Without delay, I phoned the hospital and informed the nurse now responsible for her care of my findings in addition to her primary care physician or [PCP]. Finally, I generate a memo for all staff that under no conditions may residents be allowed medications in their room unless authorized by the nurse and all medications must be taken when administered and NEVER left to a resident to self-administer.

In the days following we began to connect the dots. Ginny's appearance was apparently the result of her flushing what meals she'd been provided down her toilet, in addition to purging. [Forcing herself to throw up what food she did eat.] Marie later indicated that upon Ginny's admission she did appear slightly gaunt and to the untrained eye, her worsening was nearly imperceptible. Since the incident, we have required annual training designed to educate staff on how to identify behaviors consistent with self-harm.

Although Virginia had no known history of suicidal idealizations or previous attempts at taking her life, she'd spent many hours brooding alone in her apartment. The recent loss of her husband and subsequent relocation proved to be too much and, she understood only *one* solution. Her maladjustment nearly ended in tragedy and should serve as a wakeup call to all of us, especially the owners who no longer provide a social-services staff member and insist on operating with a skeleton crew.

Every day dozens of seniors across our nation relocate from their household following an extended hospitalization or, worse, the loss of their spouse. And while some may welcome the change assisted living has to offer, others loathe the idea and struggle to adjust. Community awareness is in need along with volunteers who can help with those wrestling with anxiety along with feelings of despair and loneliness. So many who've relocated here did so by default and live each day with false hope that someday they will—return home.

As a nurse, I've observed intentional involvement to be most effective when comforting others who now live with an ever- increasing need for assistance. Many might assume that Ginny is being closely monitored 24/7 with adequate support staff. This is simply not the case and arguably many of today's assisted living facilities are businesses that minimally assist, usually with less than adequate staff.

Another difficulty we face in AL is that residents cannot be forced to socialize, interact or otherwise get out to maintain a healthy emotional balance. In fact, we can't require residents to shower or even change their undergarment. Doing so can infringe on their rights. Short of our building being on fire, we can no more tell them they need to exit their apartment any more than we can require them to stay inside.

What we can do is encourage and educate them on the importance of getting out and socializing. For years, we had a person in social services who performed this very function. Corporate executives however eliminated this position and no doubt reallocated the revenue to other expenditures. With no additional indications from Ginny, suicide could have easily occurred. I feel blessed to have been there and made the determination that got her to the ER, but in fact I was completely unaware of her true intentions. During my nurses training, (2004-2005) seniors age sixty-five and up carried the highest rates of suicide. Little did I realize how easily it could have occurred on my watch. Tonight, I operated purely on instinct that something was wrong, but as a clinician I should have been more tuned in to my resident.

In the days following, I battled feelings of incompetence brought on by guilt and fear. Without question, I should have been more acutely aware of her situation upon my initial assessment. What I learned this night could never have been learned in any classroom or from any textbook. It tested my competence and critical thinking at a different level. The good to come out of tonight's ordeal is the need to be more keenly aware and to not be fooled in my days ahead. For weeks, I lost sleep and knew that I just needed to move on. While I feel I've come to accept my shortcomings, I'm still occasionally haunted by them.

For some elderly folks relocating to an AL facility can prove more than they can handle. A strong support network of friends and/or family is important but ongoing visits are what really help to ease feelings of loneliness and solitude. Residents are happy to be embraced by warm, friendly staff, but visitations from close friends or family always make a greater impact. If you have the chance to visit someone who has relocated to a retirement home, please find time to contact them today. It may be the last opportunity you have.

Preparation Gay

After charting, I restock my cart and begin the last of my evening rounds, starting with Edsel. Prior to leaving the clinic, I receive a call from Monique who informs me that Delores's medication arrived, which she will administer along with her other evening meds. Acknowledging the call, I arrive at Edsel's apartment. Knocking on the door, I feel my stomach growl. Once again, I have skipped dinner.

Answering the door in her multicolored seersucker housecoat is Edsel's wife, Alice. She's an adorable, petite, and balding ninety-four-year-old who's carefully watched over Edsel for nearly seventy-one years. They've lived here for as long as I can remember and rarely call for assistance. Alice has a noticeable look of worry.

"Is everything okay?" I hear groaning coming from the bedroom.

"I'm not sure." She responds in a loud whisper.

"Edsel has his hemorrhoids back…again…and after we got into bed he asked me to apply his cream … so I got up, put the light on and applied it." She hands me a tube of lotion which should have been thrown out years ago. The expiration date reads: DEC. 1971. She continues. "Well...after I got back in bed, he began groaning and complaining...saying it burns...it burns...I don't know what to do."

Straightening out the crinkled tube I notice the label to read BEN GAY! At this point I struggle with every ounce of energy to keep from laughing. Entering the bedroom, I hear his cry for relief.

"Help me...somebody please! My butts killin' me!"

Promptly, I clean off his anal area and apply the PREPARATION-H. Finally, he feels some relief and thanks me for coming to his rescue.

"That was torture cream! Next time, get somebody who knows what the hell they're doing!" He barks at his wife. Embarrassed, Alice turned slowly and exited into the living room.

A few days later I heard another resident retelling the story to friends over breakfast. She could hardly finish before the entire table erupted into uncontrollable laughter. Others seated nearby could only look on, wondering what was so funny.

In time, they'll find out as well I thought. Around here, the pace may be slow, but news travels fast; A unique yet common parallel to certain residents who either seem to always be constipated or have diarrhea.

The ladies know if you need to disseminate information quickly remember; teletype, telephone, television but most of all, tell Alice. I remember this incident whenever I hear *Ben Gay* mentioned and can't help but chuckle.

Next I head for the Rembrandt to look in on Robin. Entering, I discover the delicious smell of fresh baked brownies along with the Rat Pack music and laughter. Approaching the executive lounge, the atmosphere is rowdy. Rounding the corner, I see Robin juggling tennis balls for residents in wheelchairs, who appear amazed. Laura and Coleen are handing out the tasty warm treats along with milk while other residents dance the conga line, headed by the Troll.

I've never seen such life on our unit and am delighted to see how Robin has chosen to entertain. Like a late-night TV host, he's captured the attention of Steve and others who still have life in them and who yearn for attention. I'm impressed with his talent and want nothing more than to stay and enjoy the festivities, but I'm needed by Monique to address our problem resident Joan; who will not stop activating her call light!

Before I can answer Monique, an announcement

blares out on the overhead. Like a bull horn in everyone's ear, a pager from maintenance broadcasts a reminder regarding tonight's plumbing repairs, bringing the entertainment to a grinding halt.

"Attention all staff, in approximately fifteen minutes the water will be shut off...again the water supply will be shut off till further notice in approximately fifteen minutes...thank you!"

My immediate concern is for residents needing to be toileted before bedtime and that all toilets have fresh sanitizer tabs. Last month we were without water for nearly twelve hours following a shutoff and the odor was overwhelming. Coleen and Laura assure me that all our soakers are dry and housekeeping has replaced a number of blue sanitizer tabs this morning. As the music and dancing start back up, I head for the exit.

Back in the Van Gogh, I make a beeline for Joan's apartment. Knowing I may have words with her, my stomach tightens. By treating her with kid gloves, I've avoided what could have easily escalated to an all-out confrontation but tonight just may be the night. Since relocating here last fall, she's clearly not adjusted well to AL living. Within hours of her arrival, Joan proved to be a huge challenge to our support staff and since has remained essentially unpleasant.

Getting to know her has been impossible and even I have chosen to avoid her, which is not like me. If she doesn't have a reason to complain, then she'll find one. Joan will ring for assistance several times an hour only to state that she forgot why she called. The Marionettes have yet to address the call- light issue, and so long as she pays her bill, Joan remains in charge. Rarely is she ever seen outside her studio apartment except for meals and to get her mail. She never has any family stopover that I know of, and only once do I remember a friend ever coming to visit.

Arriving at her door I take a deep breath and again prepare to kill her with kindness. A gentle knock solicits no reply. Continuing to tap, I slowly open her door while calling her. As usual, I discover her diminutive frame sitting erect, legs crossed in her French wingback chair. Everything is rightly in its place. An unmistakable aroma permeates the air; it's that musty antique furniture odor I remember as a kid.

A tenseness fills the room with only a tiffany table lamp dimly lit in the far corner. I can *feel* her ice-blue eyes staring at me with contempt and her hair pulled back tightly, so much as to appear painful and her complexion is noticeably tan and tight, much too tight for someone of eighty-one. Angry perhaps with her appearance...I think. Previous facelifts never met her expectations and now she's forced to live with the results! I can hear in the back of my head my mom commenting that she has a *puss on her face.*

Large, nostalgic black-and-white matted family photos dominate the wall closest to her. In her prime, I can tell she was drop-dead gorgeous. One photo appeared to be of her, I don't know; I've always been too afraid to ask. If it is her, she could easily have doubled for Maureen O'Hara.

"Yes, Joan, how may I be of service?" I reach to reset her call button.

"I need a box of tissues!" she snapped in a raspy tone while clearing her throat.

"Oh look...you have a box...right here on your coffee table."

"I need more...that's only one box...I need more...now hurry up!"

"Joan...you sound a little disgruntled. Is anything wrong?" I whisper while approaching her. I kneel and gently take hold of her hands.

"Joan?"

She remains silent.

"Joan...we do all we can to please you and yet you

push us to the limit…why?"

"I don't know why!" She shot back. "Now get me some tissues!"

Suddenly a call comes for me on my radio.

"Ken…yeah it's Robin, just wanted to let you know Betty's back…from the hospital with her husband, and he needs to speak with you, when you have a minute. Oh, also, do you know where I can get a couple of D size batteries?"

"Check the activities office desk drawer, I think I saw some in there…and ah, tell Fred I'll be down shortly, please."

"Okay, thanks."

Slowly, I turned my radio volume down.

"How can I help you, Joan?" My tone is less flexible.

She continues to remain silent, looking down.

"I can't help you unless you level with me. Tell me the reason for all these call lights…if you're not careful you're going to have a heart attack…or give us one!"

Fighting her tears, she burst forth.

"I don't know…I don't know!" She squeezes my hands with full force.

"Joan…Joan, look at me…look at me, please tell me. I can't help you unless you help me by telling me what's bothering you …Joan, it's okay to speak…what's troubling you?"

"My life…my life, I was an awful mother. Nothing ever…my husband, that son of a…he left us…he left all of us. I may have wanted it but the boys, they needed him…they needed a father! Now who do I have, no one…no one! And you want to know what's wrong. Well I'm wrong, I'm wrong, I'm wrong!"

Sobbing, she allowed me to embrace her; to hold her and to *feel* her anger. I have no answers, and she doesn't want any. She needs someone to hold her, to listen to her, and to love her. I hug her with full embrace. I finally broke through.

It suddenly occurred to me what she feared most—going to the grave without sharing about her past with someone; but not just anyone and until tonight, she just couldn't find that someone. I felt honored that she chose me of all workers. I was now a therapist to a deeply troubled soul and although I encouraged counseling and therapy, she remained adamantly opposed.

As nurses, we wear many hats and are often having to try on new ones regardless of how uncomfortable they may feel. Tonight's encounter opened my eyes to how some of us live each day while quietly suffering the memories of a dark past.

Some people are just hard to love and until we understand and *feel* their pain, our ability to reach them is limited. Working here has proven to be bittersweet for me and has taught me that each of us has the ability to help others in ways that we may not be aware of. I interrogated Joan but only secondary to intervening for my staff, not out of genuine concern for Joan's well-being.

For Joan, I know it removed an enormous emotional weight off her shoulders. A lesson I learned from someone I *learned* to love.

She Dye

Back at the Rembrandt, I encounter Ralph from maintenance. He informs me our water should be restored within an hour or so, but he makes no promises. Also, a water leak is discovered near the utility closet opposite my office; orange cones identify the area.

"Yeah, that carpet's pretty soaked where I got it marked off. I'll get the heavy stuff up with my extractor, if I can get it started. We just need to put some fans here to have it dry by morning, hopefully before corporate arrives.

"Corporate is going to be here?

"Yeah, didn't you hear?

"We talked about it in standup, but I didn't know it was tomorrow."

"That's the memo we got, tomorrow sometime in the am."

His cellphone rings, and he steps away. As I head to the lounge, Coleen approaches with Fred, who's pushing Betty in a wheelchair. He hands me a manila envelope which contains Betty's discharge paperwork. I explain in further detail the fiasco which occurred earlier and take a moment to welcome her back.

"How are you?...It's good to see you back."

All she can offer is an exhausted smile. Fred pipes in.

"Yeah, the doc said—as far as he can see—that her heart returned to normal and to just keep an eye on her. She seems to be doing fine although she hasn't eaten anything except a spoonful of yogurt. I'm just going to lay her down to rest."

"That's probably what she needs most. I'm glad she's doing better. In case she does get hungry, we have stuff here also—bananas, half sandwiches, and yogurt. Coleen will help with getting her to bed and will also get her vitals; just watch that area. We've got a water leak."

As they roll away, I review the discharge paperwork before radioing Robin, who assures me everything is fine.

"Most have gone to bed but a few are still up." He answers, and I hear Marvin Gaye music in the background. The transmission is partially broken by Monique who's also attempting to reach me. Her second effort reveals that Sam has returned with his niece and wishes to have his blood sugar taken. I radio I'll be there in a few minutes, after my rounds in the Rembrandt. My first concern is Steve and how he's adjusting.

Arriving at his apartment, I peer in to see him resting peacefully. Next, I'm on to the lounge area to check in on Robin when I see Fred nearing the exit. Knowing he'll need to be let out, I detour after him. Disarming the door, I notice the elevator open and Merri step off. She approaches carrying an overnight shave kit. Before I can introduce her to Fred, she hands me the worn travel kit embroidered with an American Airlines emblem next the words CAPTAIN STEVE.

"I forgot to bring this."

"Oh okay, I'll take it in to him…Merri, this is Fred."

"Hi, how are you?" Fred offers his hand with a gentle nod.

"Good." She extends for a nervous shake before turning back to me.

"How's he doing?"

"Great, he's doing great. He was in the lounge earlier enjoying the music and karaoke, and now he's sleeping. If you want, you can sneak a peek."

"No, that's okay, I was just curious." She gives a sigh of relief.

"How is your granddaughter?"

"Good. They say it's meningitis.

"Do you know what kind?"

"Yes, viral. They have her on IV fluids and say her temperature has stabilized.

"How old is she?"

"Twenty. We're just glad they caught it early. Steve just adores her. I'm sure you'll get to meet her after she's better. We're hoping to have her home in a day or two. So Steve's doing okay . . . you feel?"

"Did he ask about me, after I left?"

"He didn't ask me, but he may have asked Laura or Coleen."

Fred interjects. "Is this his first day?"

"Yes." Answers Merri.

Knowing it's my opportunity to duck out, I cut in. "Merri, I'm going to take this to his room. If either of you need me, just notify one of the aids and they'll page me, thanks."

They both nod and continue conversing as I turn to disarm the door. I feel good, knowing that Fred is probably the best companion for Merri right now. Introducing family members is therapeutic on so many levels. Emotional support is shared, especially for spouses who may be new to the whole memory unit setting. Reentering, I run into Laura, who is walking with Betty.

"I thought Coleen laid her down."

"Yes, that's what I thought too, but I found her in her doorway asking for Fred. I tried to lay her back down but, she wasn't having it…so we're taking a little walk."

Coleen rounds the corner and offers the same surprised look. "I just laid her down." She announces with a chuckle. Betty smiles.

"Can you do me a favor please?" I ask. "See if she'll tolerate staying in a wheelchair and take this shaving kit to Steve's room. Thanks, I've gotta check Sam's blood sugar."

"Sure thing."

"Oh, Robin's still doing okay?", I asked.

"Yes, he's awesome. They're all slow dancing now. He's really got it going on." They giggle.

"I know, I saw him juggling earlier."

"Yeah, but now he's got quite the *setup* back there."

"Set up?"

"A dance floor with lights and everything." They answer.

"What?"

"Yeah, you should check it out. He was even doing cartwheels."

"Cartwheels!"

"Yeah, and back flips."

"Backflips!" I yell. Laura and Coleen laugh.

Before I can get to the lounge area, Monique calls me on my radio.

"We need a blood sugar check please…family members are waiting…thank you!"

Unable to see Robin's gig, I begrudgingly head for the Van Gogh. Exiting, I pass Fred and Merri, still conversing by the elevator. Arriving at the nurse's station I discover Monique laughing with Sam and Missy, Sam's niece, who seems to visit only when she's low on funds.

Suddenly we hear a loud crack of thunder followed by the lights flickering. The momentary darkness brings complete silence.

"Uh oh!" Sam breaks the quiet. "Hope we don't have a repeat of last night."

Sam rolls into the nurse's station as I check my flashlight.

"Hey!" He announces. "We just got back from dinner."

"Okay, how was it?" Finally, my flash light is working.

"Great…except we waited for nearly an hour for a table and I'm curious what my blood sugar reading might be…can you check it now?"

"Absolutely." I reach for his test kit. "How late was it?"

"Oh…we ate about seven forty-five or so." He looks at Missy.

"Yeah, it's almost nine now and, you're due to be checked now anyway." I say trying not to stare at Missy. Tonight, with Missy it's all gold—jewelry, clothes, nails, hair, makeup and even contact lenses…all the glitter.

"So…what's his numb-ah?" she asks cracking her gum.

"Just one more moment and we'll have it. So, where did you guys eat?"

"We went to that Barnard's Blue Crab down on Main." Sam answers. "It was crowded, but we had a wonderful time, I got their lobster bisque and coconut crusted mahi mahi…man was it good!"

"That sounds delicious; and your sugar looks good…only one fifty-one. Just a couple of units of coverage will do."

Administering his insulin, I feel Missy's eyes, micromanaging my every move. Soon they're headed down the hall to his room. Fearing a power outage, I re-attempt to contact Delores's great-grandson. Answering on the first ring, I attempt to identify who I am when I'm met with a loud, thick Southern drawl.

"She die?"

I'm speechless. "Uh…no sir, she's okay…she's been prescribed additional medication for fluid retention." I can't believe he just said that…I think. Sheepishly he responded.

"Oh…well okay…what's wrong with her again?"

In layman's terms, I explained how the medication is needed to alleviate her swollen ankles, and to avoid more serious complications such as pneumonia.

"She got pneumonia?" he snapped back.

"No sir, she does not have pneumonia." I answered while kicking myself. "She only has some mild swelling around her ankles and she's been prescribed medication to correct it…she's doing fine right now and is resting soundly in her room. If you like, I can have her call you when she wakes up?"

"Oh…okay well she ain't gotta call me…but if she restin'… that's good."

I assured him that in the days following we would provide updates as to her status.

Monique entered the nurse's station laughing hysterically. "Did he just ask you if she died?"

"Yes, can you believe it?!" I chuckle.

Apparently, he spoke so loud, she could hear him from outside the nurse's station.

"And can you believe how Missy was dressed?" she says in a gossipy whisper.

"I know…sure are some interesting people out there. I'm going to call for an update on Calvin and check on Delores. Call if you need me."

"Will do."

My call to the ER gets me an operator who pages Calvin's nurse. What I hear is shocking.

"He's been stable since leaving critical care and right now he's enjoying a bowl of ice-cream. Doctor Williams may even discharge him later tonight. What number can I reach you at?"

I provide her my direct line and cell number before hanging up. Next I complete a chart note on the update while wondering how Calvin could have rebounded so quickly. Sometimes I'm taken by surprise by what my residents do, especially ones like Calvin whom I've grown to love over the years.

Oldie but Goodie

Before returning to the Rembrandt, I stop to check on Delores. Quietly entering her room, I discover her sleeping peacefully in the recliner. Due to her age, I find myself checking on her more often. I pause briefly to stare at her chest and feel relieved as I note the subtle up and down motion. During my tenure, I've discovered two residents deceased who appeared to be sleeping so I always confirm chest movement.

Exiting, I glance at the half-opened door across the hall, marked 319, the apartment now sits empty. Over the years, Delores has survived so many of her neighbors, I've lost count. All the names and faces now gone—but not forgotten. Bob will always remain with me. He was an oldie but goodie, and I'm privileged to have known him.

He came to us late one Friday following his discharge from rehab. The previous month he'd undergone an open-heart procedure known as a CABG (Coronary

Artery Bypass Graph) pronounced cabbage. His collaborative-care team determined that AL would be an appropriate level of assistance for him in addition to receiving physical and occupational therapy. An alumnus of Harvard, he held graduate degrees in both chemistry and mathematics which his children and grandchildren proudly displayed in his hallway along with other family photos.

Over my career, I've discovered a small percentage of seniors who will never be the same after undergoing general anesthesia. This was the case with Bob.

After completing my initial assessment, I spoke with his family, who confirmed my suspicion that cognitively, he had taken a big step down. We were happy to have him under our care. He was adored by our staff and loved by his fellow residents. Fortunately, his sense of humor was not affected, and often he would have those him around in stitches. Among a few other geriatric jokers here he could always be counted on for funny one liners. 319 became his new home over the following ten months but after his memory began to fail, the Rembrandt is where he would live out his final and most memorable days.

His looks were a cross between Walt Disney and Walter Cronkite, complete with receding hairline and carefully cropped mustache. His suspenders always appeared uneven and often twisted which he insisted on not correcting. He and Delores soon became close friends and would often be found working jigsaw puzzles together in his apartment. His witty sense of humor and loveable disposition caused him to quickly become a favorite amongst everyone. Following his admission, he insisted on being called Bob "Newheart."

In his bedroom hung his wedding photo and was the only picture of his late bride, Juanita. As high-school sweethearts they were engaged after graduating and married over Thanksgiving weekend—the Sunday before Pearl Harbor. They were in Niagara Falls the morning of the attack and he said he could remember it like it was yesterday. During lunch a kitchen worker bolted into the dining area shouting…

…"The Japanese bombed Pearl Harbor…The Japanese bombed Pearl Harbor!"

Most looked around, repeating, "Where's Pearl Harbor?"

The wedding shot of Juanita reminded me of Alice on the Honeymooners and while discussing his wall of photos, he spoke very little of her except to say how she met her fate. Tragically she was killed by a drunk driver on New Year's Eve 1963, only hours before I was born.

I never shared with him about it being the eve of my birthday. I'd always felt too guilty.

An oversized and luxurious suite, 319 featured a large bay window overlooking a lake teeming with wild-life. Within a year however, he was relocated to our Rembrandt for safety concerns. He'd wandered into the shallows at the far end of the lake and was found holding a turtle, unable to recall how he'd gotten there. After his move to memory care, my coworkers and I really took to him, learning more of his past and on occasion escorting him back to the pond where he enjoyed being a kid again.

Early one spring Saturday, I took off work and brought in fishing poles and sandwiches. With the morning sun on our backs, we cast our lines and shared our past. For a moment, I was back on the farm in Maryland where I grew up. Bob repeated himself while struggling to cast his line. Setting my pole aside, I began to help him as he told me about his life.

Although he never shared exactly what his job entailed, it was rumored that he'd worked on the Manhattan Project. He mentioned a place called Twenty-Five Broadway, a secret location where he was assigned for a short time before heading out west. I couldn't help but think about his contribution to our country and our allies. Like Oppenheimer and the others, he helped end the war using only his brain...and a chalkboard. How many people can say that?! I truly felt honored to be with him and to hear his perspective on how things have changed—once the atom was split; An important lesson on history and when to listen closely to our elders.

By late afternoon we hadn't even caught a single fish and I soon realized that neither of us were really there to fish. Gathering up our rods, cooler and tackle boxes something began moving in the bushes. Curious, Bob decided to check it out. Carefully, he bent over and took hold of a large turtle crawling in the thicket. He said it was a male due to his long tail and concave indent on his underbelly.

"He needs that indent for mating...otherwise he might fall off at the moment of truth! Bob bellowed.

I doubled over with laughter as Bob returned the turtle to the water's edge. Walking at Bob's pace, we moseyed around the perimeter of the lake, enjoying the fresh air and wild life. I wanted to tell him he was the granddad I never had, but feeling weird about it decided not to. Looking back, I wish I had. Back at the Rembrandt, he thanked me and hugged me.

"You're a good guy." He said; "And about a good a

fisherman as I am." We chuckled. It was a day I'll never forget and one I'd wish we'd done more often.

On other days, I would quiz Bob with the use of flashcards and marveled at his ability to recall long term. Despite his struggles with short-term memory (STM), he was able without hesitation, to match nearly all elements on the periodic table to their corresponding symbols and numbers.

Throughout the day, though, he would be seen wandering the halls looking for his room. Bob's inability to recall short-term demonstrates how AD can annihilate certain areas of the brain while regions responsible for long-term memory (LTM) remain healthy.

I've discovered this to be common for many in the initial to moderate stages of the disease and is why I focus so much on learning their history. It's my way to connect with them before they begin to undergo significant changes and fully fall victim to the disease.

Like with many other residents, a great deal of my interaction with Bob occurred at the wagon as I handed out medications. He always stuttered a joke or riddle with us while waiting for his pills. Looking back, I now realize what little time I had with Bob was truly special. The day we spent at the lake remains my favorite time with him. He acted to bring out the best in others and at times appeared almost too good to be in a locked unit. Eager to help, he would often assist with pouring juice and handing out snacks in late afternoon. His own favorite treat happened to be chocolate-covered peanuts, which he often enjoyed while playing checkers with other residents who could function at his level. On more than one occasion I noticed him helping his opponent and soon realized exactly what type of guy he was.

Following his move to the Rembrandt, he'd lost a great deal of weight and had to be refitted with new clothes. One afternoon during our Karaoke Hour, his pants fell while he was crooning to "Luck be a Lady" from <u>Guys and Dolls</u>. As expected most other residents in attendance hardly took notice until he announced boldly into the microphone…"My pants just fell down!"

Suddenly all eyes were on him including one employee who laughed so hard she peed on herself.

Bob inspired other residents to escape their comfort zone and live each day to its fullest. He enjoyed leading them in such favorites as the Hokey Pokey and the Chicken Dance during activities hour and often entertained us with his own infamous dance moves. Twisting and turning his hips, he was all the entertainment we needed. He never posed a problem or asked for anything. He truly was a rarity.

The following spring, he was admitted to a Cardiac Care Unit for chest pain. I remember the emptiness we all felt after he was gone. The Rembrandt just wasn't the same and as employees, we eagerly awaited his return. While in the hospital, his prognosis dwindled with each day and upon his readmission to the Rembrandt, he was placed on Hospice.

Although wheelchair bound, he managed throughout the day to self-propel around the unit. Occasionally he would need a push to get over a doorway threshold or around furniture. He was undergoing the painful lesson of losing his independence, and over time I found myself helping him—to a fault. I was doing him a disservice by helping him. Offering too much assistance says more about me (guilt) than it does about Bob really needing help. During this transition phase, he was having to let go, and so was I.

After several months, Bob became bed fast and his last weeks I spent with him were at meal times and during visits with hospice personnel. By now he was slow to answer questions but still enjoyed a good joke. Up until the end, he loved to make others laugh.

His celestial discharge came on a rainy afternoon in August. I remember feeling as though a part of me was suddenly *gone.* In those few precious moments of his passing, I was reminded of the choices I'd made earlier in my life; choices that resulted in wasted opportunities like watching TV instead of watching the sunset or making time to be with family, or just fishing.

After he was pronounced, I exited the crowded room. I only looked down as I quickly headed for my car before letting go. It was in my early years when I was still too proud to openly show my emotions. Little did I know how Bob's death would mark the beginning of a long career spent comforting others—facing their end. His passing was perhaps the hardest "on the job training" I've ever had to undergo and yet the most meaningful. I can still hear his laugh.

In the days that followed I began to reflect about my past and more importantly, how I would choose to invest my days ahead. I found myself thinking about Bob while at work and especially at the wagon. Of all the residents, I've grown to love, Bob was perhaps the hardest to say goodbye to. I'll always be forced to remember August 5th with sadness. Becoming attached to certain residents is unavoidable, and my coworkers and I experienced painful emotions brought about by the suffering and death of those taken by the ravages of old age.

We count on each other for support. After losing Bob I found myself in a funk for several days. My emotional struggles eased over time with the support of Tina and the others. We would talk after work sometimes and laughter became our best therapy.

Over the years, I've seen dozens of individuals come and go. Some were retired state Supreme Court justices, container-ship captains and university presidents. Others were stay-at-home moms, missionaries and former FBI Agents. Each move-in is a new opportunity to listen and learn the details of how others lived and what lessons they've learned. Questions I've added to the psychological/social portion of our intake include;

"If you could live your life over…what would you have done differently?"

"The greatest thing I'm thankful for is…"

"If you didn't know how old you were, how old would you be?"

"When I'm gone, I want to be remembered for…"

Often responses come after a period of extended silence as they ponder their past. Over time, especially as they begin to face end of life, they don't feel threatened by what others may think of them and consequently…open up. Good listening skills become my greatest asset.

Age has a way of refining us. It erodes the bravado until our deepest inner being is exposed. It evidences at our core, we're all the same; Individuals who yearn for companionship and whose greatest fear is being of no use to others and who end up…alone.

The greatest generation, the world may ever know
Now lives alone in a nursing home,
with nowhere left to go
Down lonely halls behind apartment walls
they lay and watch T.V.
Hoping for a friend to visit, someone like you or me
Each day begins with nurse's aides,
who help to clean and dry
After breakfast is a doctor's visit,
a long white coat and tie
Wondering what the day will bring,
they lie awake in bed
Hoping for the phone to ring, while waiting on their meds
After dinner is a gameshow winner,
before drifting off to sleep
This is how they are now,
but may one day be you or me
So clean your hide and dump your pride,
tomorrow ever near
If you learn to be humble, your ego will tumble
and with age you'll have less fear.

Humble Pie

After finishing my rounds in the Van Gogh, I head for the Rembrandt to see the dance floor Robin has fashioned. Enroute, Ruth approaches pushing her walker as though she's late for an appointment. All smiles, she's up and at 'em.

"Good morning!" she announces. Monique rounds the corner and together we attempt to redirect her.

"Honey, it's ten o'clock at night." Monique says, attempting to redirect her.

"Are you sure?"

"Yes." I say "See my watch…it's ten o'clock."

"Here, hon I'll help you back to your apartment, okay?"

Ruth looked confused as Monique gently turned her walker, and escorted her back home. Those who struggle with their circadian rhythm or sleep/wake cycle typically make up between one to two percent of our residents. In all my years, I've yet to identify exactly why some fall victim to this sleep malady, and others do not. A condition common for some in which they flip their internal day/night time frame and thus, show for breakfast at improper times. Cat naps during the day no doubt worsen this syndrome and some who suffer from this type of "silver insomnia" appear to run a greater risk of ending up in the Rembrandt.

Only an hour or so into their sleep, they awake to begin what they think is the start of their day. After showering, dressing, inserting dentures, teasing hair, applying makeup, and adorning themselves with their finest jewelry, they head for the dining room only to be promptly redirected back to their apartment. Despite numerous reminders, they may repeat this pattern several times during the same night. Generally, it's not considered a safety concern unless they begin to wander with no understood destination. Should this occur, their eagerness to "exit seek" will most likely follow and proper interventions must be taken.

For those of us who are not yet seniors, we can plan for just how we will adjust to these unfortunate changes which often come with age. Eventually, we will ALL likely face the need to be cared for by others and the time to start preparing for this life lesson is now. This includes not only getting our affairs in order but also preparing for what emotional and psychological challenges we'll likely face. As we grow older, many of us are faced with very difficult and expensive decisions. Decisions which greatly impact our future quality of life.

My vocation as a nurse goes far beyond taking temperatures and giving pills. Nursing has allowed me the chance to minister to families facing the challenges of placing a loved one into AL or memory care; helping others find hope when all appears lost is a challenge not found in many of today's career fields.

For me, this is the most rewarding and recognizable accomplishment I can achieve and is at the very heart of nursing. The love, support, compassion, encouragement, and accountability we demonstrate toward others describes not only who we are as employees but more importantly defines our true character.

A great way to get acquainted with this reality is to volunteer at a local hospital or nursing home. I received just a taste of this type of this humility years ago, while in nurses training. What we thought was going to be a lesson on bedside manner turned out to be an experience none of us would soon forget. As students, we were taught the importance of understanding care from the patients' perspective.

During the portion of our training which involved the use of bedpans, we were divided up into small groups. Each group had a leader whom the other group members elected. The leader was to select one group participant to poop into the bed pan, and another to empty it. As one of the group leaders what I remember most is how red some of my fellow student's faces became, including mine!

Of course, dividing up into groups was as far as we got but the lesson was powerful. As most would guess, all who volunteered were willing to empty the pan but no one could endure the humiliation needed to defecate into it. Without question the exercise gave each of us a lasting impression of exactly how humbling it can feel while depending on others for assistance.

On the resident side of the equation is the painful lesson of learning humility. My tenure as a nurse has taught me that for some, learning to graciously accept help from others can be emotionally sobering for at least two reasons:

First, is physical and involves the slow and painful process of losing one's independence. This ranges from having to relinquish driving privileges, to requiring assistance while toileting. Residents here struggle to perform simple tasks which for years, they easily performed on their own;

Second, is the psychological toll which serves as a healthy dose of humility, thus driving out any pride and self-sufficiency. These paradigms can be overwhelming for some and care must be taken to see that they are able to adapt. Making conversation while assisting with personal care is one way to help residents feel more comfortable. Over the years, I've learned an important lesson strictly through observation; all may appear well on the outside but deep inside—they may be nervous, embarrassed and in some cases angry.

When we're young, we simply don't think much about the need to humbly accept help from others or what future independence/pride issues await us. As a rule, it's easier to offer help—than to receive it.

Over my tenure, I've had the privilege of comforting dozens of individuals. Many just needed a listening ear; others battled feelings of loneliness and some were just simply, scared to die. To hold their hand while reassuring them is where I'm needed most in my line of work and is of immeasurable value to those suffering. Nursing has taught me to serve in some of the greatest ways possible and has forced me to consider what future struggles I may someday face.

Labor of Love

Entering the Rembrandt, a loud clap of thunder drowns out Captain Kangaroo's hourly chime and now we have it—a total power failure. I reach for my flashlight while thinking about the electronic door behind me. Without power, it cannot lock! I radio my staff to monitor the halls for residents caught in the dark. Monique informs me her flashlight is dim but, for now she can get by.

I assign Laura to act as the door watchman and ask Coleen to make rounds while pushing Betty in her wheelchair. Coleen acknowledges when suddenly we hear a noise. Someone is approaching. Peering through the dark we discover Steve, who apparently has awakened and looks in no mood to negotiate.

"How, how do I get out of here?" He stutters angrily.

Surprisingly, Betty pipes in. "You're not going anywhere hon, this is where we live."

Speechless, Coleen and I stare at each other wondering if Betty can redirect Steve. Awaiting his response, I can feel his silent serious stare. Coleen attempts to reorient him.

"Yeah, Steve, this where you live. Remember putting your clothes away with me? Let me help you get back." She extends her hand, and Betty follows, extending hers slightly farther. Reluctantly, he accepts only Betty's hand before beginning to walk.

As they head down the hall, I can tell he's wondering who Betty is but isn't sure of what to do. For appearing tough, it's now as though he's scared to even ask a question. Relieved, I watch them roll toward the lounge area before heading to my office to search for batteries.

From down the hall, I hear Mr. Robinson's cry. The last crack of thunder and subsequent blackout have him noticeably worried, and entering my office, I find him crouched atop his file cabinet, meowing. I do my best to console him before locating one new and one used battery. Also, I grab a Coleman lantern from under my desk. Next, I attempt to call Marge downstairs, but the rapid busy signal indicates our phones are also out.

After I hang up, Mr. Robinson suddenly leaps into my lap and presses his paws against my chest, as though commandeering me to do something about tonight's problems. Great I think, stroking his sweet spot. What if

I should have to call 911? With a reassuring hug, I relocate him back on top of the file cabinet before trying my cell, which nets me no bars. Grabbing my lantern, I exit the office, hoping to get better reception elsewhere. Arriving at the entrance, I see Laura leaning against the doors, holding them shut.

"How long you think we'll be without power?"

I can tell she's not exactly thrilled about being door watchman. "I'm not sure...but with any luck, we should have generator power soon...I tried Marge but couldn't get through."

"Oh yeah." She says. "I keep hearing this weird knocking coming from the stairwell next to the elevator...I can't figure out what's causing it."

"Where?"

"Right there." She points to the far wall between the elevator and stairwell exit.

"Yeah sure." I head that way when suddenly we hear laughter and commotion coming from back in the Rembrandt. Driven by curiosity, I motion to Laura I'll be right back before doing an about-face to penetrate the blackness with my trusty Coleman.

Nearing the executive lounge, the odor of incense once again apprehends my nose, and rounding the corner I discover a night club atmosphere with residents laughing, dancing, and congregating around the wagon. Borrowing from the activities closet, Robin has managed to transform the entire lounge area into a quasi-Studio 54 discothèque. Several residents including, Steve and Betty, are slow dancing to Sexual Healing on a makeshift dance floor complete with overhead mirrored ball, black lights, and Bluetooth Surround Sound. Puzzled as to how he's managed power, I note his laser pen taped to the wall thermostat and pointed toward our mirrored ball, which I recall has a windup feature. Several half-empty bake pans litter the lounge area along with crumpled milk cartons and dirty napkins.

Behind the wagon, he's clearly the center of attention. As tonight's master of ceremony, Robin's attire consists of Emma's silver fox, a pair of wraparound cataract sunglasses, and an oversized purple hat with pink fringe that reads *PIMP DADDY!* With his iPhone, he has become tonight's DJ and card dealer for residents around the wagon, which now doubles as a blackjack table. Groovin' to the Motown, he has all the moves and appeal of a modern-day Wolf Man Jack, but with a heart for those here in lockdown. OMG I think…what if the marionettes see this? Speechless, I head for the wagon when I receive a radio call from Laura.

"Aaah…can you come back here…to the entrance

please, now? I kinda got a situation."

"Sure, I'll be right there."

Chuckling, I quickly head back. Approaching the entrance, I hear Laura and Coleen trying to redirect the Troll away from workers entering with tools and equipment.

"What's that thing?" barks the Troll.

"We use it to clean up water spills." Answers a maintenance worker.

"You say you were gonna give me my pills?"

"No, ma'am." Laughs Ralph.

Suddenly we have power and the overheads blind us.

"Haaaay!" everyone cheers.

Generators provide us a reprieve from the darkness and finally we can stash our flashlights. The Troll is pretending to appear interested in Ralph and the workers but is really looking for the chance to elope. Escorting her from the entrance, I leave her with Coleen when I receive a broken radio call from Monique regarding Missy (Sam's niece), who demands to know when the power will be restored. We hear her anger in stereo over our radios except mine which is beeping, and my low batt light is flashing.

"When are you all going to turn the lights back on?"

"My uncle needs to see to go to the bathroom...you

need to get here …NOW!"

Ralph and the others look at me as if to say…what is she talking about…they are back on…oh well…glad it's you and not me. He and his workers continue trying to start the extractor.

"On my way," I answer while grabbing my Coleman and the batteries I stashed earlier. Entering the Van Gogh, I'm back in the dark. Arriving at the nurse's station, I ask Monique to fill a bedpan with water from the ice machine in the kitchen and warm it up on the gas stove. "Bring it down to Sam's room as soon as you can, please. I've got to go deal with Missy."

Once in Sam's room, I place my Coleman atop Sam's chest of drawers as Missy starts in on me.

"Why don't they have more help around here?" she demanded. "And what's going on…no water…no power…you know he pays over six grand a month to live here…this is a bunch of bull!"

"I'm sorry…I'll get him cleaned up now."

Sam hung his head as Missy continued her rant. Monique arrives with the bed pan, and together we worked on Sam.

"I don't understand why you people don't do your job!" Missy continued angrily.

As we proceed with her uncle's care, she began to

soften her tone, taking notice of our gentleness while changing his undergarment and carefully wiping his private area.

"I don't know why they don't hire more help around here!" she continued, cracking her gum. "They'd better hire some more help or I'm pulling my dad out of here, this is awful...who do I contact about this?" she demanded, holding her iPhone.

I quickly jotted down Carol and Marie's contact information in addition to our complaint resolution department email. Handing Missy the information, I notice the Troll has entered the room with her walker and is staring intently at Missy. Before I can talk, the Troll begins interrogating Missy.

"What time you gonna give me my pills?"

Missy looks up at the Troll, and Monique spins around with a look of disbelief.

"I don't have your pills, honey." Missy responds, staring at her iPhone.

"How did you get out here?" Monique interjects.

"Alright, well don't forget...I'll be in bed." Responds the Troll, ignoring Monique.

"What did you say?" The Troll blurts, pretending not to understand Missy.

Monique tries not to chuckle.

"How did you get out here?" Monique asks again. "Never mind, come on, let's go!"

As Monique and the Troll headed out, I gathered up dirty linens before emptying the bedpan. I notice Missy standing with her arms folded, and a look of disgust. An awkward silence and foul smell of feces permeates the room. I can't wait to escape.

"Thank you for cleaning my uncle" she says in an apologetic tone. "I'm sorry I got so upset but, I just...I just feel he deserves better care than this." She wipes her tears. "I'm sure you can understand how I feel . . . can't you?"

"Yes, I do...and you're absolutely right." I continue while unfolding a clean pair of pajamas from Sam's closet. "We try our hardest to give the best possible care but are often shorthanded and on a night like tonight, it's tough. I personally will do my best to keep a close eye on your uncle and with your permission, will forward your phone number to my supervisors. We're struggling with our staffing numbers and have needed additional help for some time. I want management to hear from you...then maybe things will change." Not sure what to say next, I remain silent and endure a period of quiet awkwardness.

"I'll get these on him." she says while reaching for his

pajamas.

"Are you sure? Cause, I can do it."

"No, really, it's fine." She responds. "You've done so much already. Thank you for tending to my uncle so quickly." She continues helping her uncle lift his arms into his pajama top.

"Thank you for all you've done. I'll be in touch" she says with a brief smile.

Over the years, I've noticed residents' family members are reluctant to voice their concerns. Causing too much of a fuss may result in having to relocate their loved one to another facility.

Aside from certain behavioral difficulties, such as violent aggression, this is rarely, if ever, the case.

When considering placement of a loved one into a facility, whether it be independent living, assisted living, skilled nursing or memory care unit, always begin by asking the staff if they are dedicated to serving the management and always finish by asking the management if they value their staff. Any hesitation is a dead giveaway.

Overtired Under Fire

Returning to the Rembrandt, I quickly check the halls and find Delores standing in her doorway wanting to know why the lights don't work. I explain about the outage and help her to the bathroom.

"I'll come and let you know when the powers back on, otherwise how are you doing?" I ask.

"What did you say?"

After repeating myself, she responds.

"Well, at least I'm still vertical…some of the time." She says with a chuckle while positioning her bum on the toilet. I love her sense of humor. Afterwards, I change her undergarment and help her get situated back in her chair. I tell her our call light system is down and I'll check back again as soon as I can. Graciously she thanked me and told me I was her favorite. Blushing, I didn't know what to say other than thank you.

After a gentle hug, I quickly head back to the Rembrandt. Exiting the stairwell, I hear the strange tapping sound Laura spoke of earlier. I listen carefully but am unable to determine its source. I radio for maintenance but get no response. I reattempt with my cell but, no signal. Discouraged, I head for the Rembrandt. Arriving, I feel a large pit in my stomach when I notice both entrance doors hanging wide open with no one in sight except Mr. Robinson, twitching his tail.

Outside my office, I encounter Ralph and his crew still fiddling with the primitive oversized water extractor. One worker in overalls, grossly overweight and in need of a shower, anxiously approaches with a worried look. On his hat are the words "*Git er done.*"

"You got an extension cord, sir?"

"Maybe in there." I point to the utility closet.

Arriving at the executive lounge, I discover it to be quiet, with residents snoring and passed out on the couch and E-Z chairs, but no sign of Robin. Heading back, I radio for anyone, but still hear nothing. Passing Betty's room, I glance in and notice her to be spooning with Steve in her bed. Great I think, what's Merri going to say if she sees that? Continuing toward the entrance, I remember my radio's low battery light and run to my office for a charger. Rounding the corner, I see the Troll pestering several maintenance workers who are trying to start the shop vac Robin and I stashed earlier.

"No!" I shout. "That's already full!"

"What the heck's going on here?" I hear from behind

me. Standing in the entryway are Carol, Marie, both state inspectors and our corporate regional director, Dick. Before I can speak, the shop vac's blower motor starts with the Troll in command of its nozzle.

"What time are you going to give me my pills?" she shouts pointing it at Carol and the others. Like a 1920's gangster she lets em' have it, firing thousands of medication tablets.

"Hit the deck!" I yell. Ralph and his workers fight the Troll for control of the hose as Mr. Robinson high tails it down the hall. Finally, "Git er done" pulls the plug and following the mayhem, Robin appears with Laura, Coleen and Monique.

"Where were you?!" I ask.

"Downstairs with EMS/FIRE. Didn't you hear us? We've been calling you for over half an hour."

"My battery ran low, I should have realized that sooner."

Emergency personnel enter and tend to those with the more serious wounds, caused mostly by the bullet-shaped suppositories and liquid-filled gel caps. Soon all are headed to the ER.

"I want a complete report of this on my desk by morning," Carol growled, heading for the ambulance.

"What was EMS here for?" I ask Laura.

"Two people were trapped in the elevator, some man and a lady. They said they banged on the wall for hours...rumor had it they were spooning when EMS opened the door."

Laura and Coleen exit my office as the phone rings.

"Hi it's Marge. Jason and the others from the overnight shift called and said they're going to be late. Apparently, the streets are flooded and trees are down everywhere. The good news is we have power restored to both the Rembrandt and Van Gogh and the call light system is back up and running."

"Great! Thanks for the update. Did they say how late they would be?" I ask.

"They weren't able to say but judging on how bad the roads are probably...at least an hour or two."

"Alright, I'll just have to stay over until someone arrives. Please give me a call when they get here."

"Sure thing."

"Thanks."

I've got a lot to say to Robin but right now I'm too exhausted.

Completing my report for Carol, I notice the light on my phone flashing. The hour old message is from Judy, Calvin's daughter. She advises that he is now at Hospice House and will likely pass either later tonight or early tomorrow. Also, she expresses her gratitude for the care we provided him over the years and will call tomorrow with an update. I replay the message several times to satisfy my denial. Memories of Calvin flood my mind as I erase the tape. Ralph and his workers finish cleaning the mess before gathering up their equipment.

"I guess that about does it." Ralph comments resetting the entry door. "I'll see you tomorrow."

"See you tomorrow." I answer, grabbing a Kleenex. Looking up, I see the Troll now standing in my doorway. Ironic I think as this is how my day started. With her eyes half closed, she is too tired to ask about her pills.

"You've had a long day. I'll bet you are ready to hit the sack." I say before blowing my nose.

She stands quietly rubbing her eyes. Like a child, she wishes to be put to bed with her nightly drink of water. Gently, I guide her toward her room and help to toilet her. After providing her a small drink of water, I tuck her into bed.

Kneeling at her side, I pray and thank God for giving me the opportunity to care for her, and for so many others over the years. I still cannot believe Calvin is gone to Hospice House.

Without a word, she gives me a warm smile and closes her eyes. I kiss her forehead and bid her good night. As frustrating as she can be at times, she needs someone to provide for her and love her like family; tonight, *I* am her family.

Captain Kangaroo sounds one AM as I relocate the last chart from my desk to the shelf. Bushed, I retire to the entrance in my oversized vinyl office chair. I'm now the door man until more staff arrives. I rest my eyes for only a moment when suddenly the alarm sounds and Mr. Robinson is again on my chest. The overnight crew has arrived and following report I replenish Mr. Robinsons' food and water. With achy joints and a mild headache, I'm on to the breakroom to punch out. My day is not yet finished.

Exiting the parking lot, I head for Hospice House. I just hope I'm not too—*late.*

About the Author

K. Allen is a License Practical Nurse who specializes in behavioral modification and interactive caregiving. He resides in South West Florida with his wife and teenage son.

52801956R00105

Made in the USA
San Bernardino, CA
29 August 2017